Millionaire
in Command

CATHERINE MANN

MILLS & BOON®

JUL 14 2010

First published in Great Britain 2010
Large Print edition 2010
Harlequin Mills & Boon Limited,
Eton House, 18-24 Paradise Road,
Richmond, Surrey TW9 1SR

© Catherine Mann 2009

ISBN: 978 0 263 21575 5

Printed and bound in Great Britain
by CPI Antony Rowe, Chippenham, Wiltshire

CATHERINE MANN

RITA® Award winner Catherine Mann resides on a sunny Florida beach with her military flyboy husband and their four children. Although after nine moves in twenty years, she hasn't given away her winter gear! With over a million books in print in fifteen countries, she has also celebrated five RITA® Award finals, three Maggie Award of Excellence finals and a Booksellers' Best win.

A former theatre school director and university teacher, she graduated with a master's degree in theatre from UNC-Greensboro and a bachelor's degree in fine arts from the College of Charleston. Catherine enjoys hearing from readers and chatting on her message board—thanks to the wonders of the wireless Internet that allows her to cyber-network with her lap-top by the water! To learn more about her work, visit her website, www.CatherineMann.com, or reach her by snail mail at PO Box 6065, Navarre, FL 32566, USA.

All my love to my flyboy husband, Rob.
Even after many years
and four children,
you still make my heart flutter!

One

Phoebe Slater brought a baby to the millionaire military hero's seaside welcome-home gala.

Undoubtedly most of the guests plucking canapés and champagne from silver trays at this high-profile affair could afford nannies. Of course the Hilton Head Island wealthy could also afford tailored tuxedos and sequined high-end dresses as they mingled the evening away in the country club gardens by the shore. Her basic little black dress had been bought at a consignment store to wear to the few mandatory cocktail parties related to her position as a history professor at the University of South Carolina.

Of course she usually didn't accessorize with baby drool dotting her shoulder.

Phoebe jostled the fractious five-month-old infant on her hip, smoothing down the pink smocked dress. "Hang on, sweetie. Just a few more minutes and I can feed you before bedtime."

As waves crashed in the distance, a live band played oldies rock, enticing guests to the dance floor with a Billy Joel classic. Even South Carolina's governor was dancing under the silver silk canopy with his wife.

Darn near gawking, Phoebe stumbled on the edge of the flagstone walkway.

Definitely this was a party for the movers and shakers in the political world—as well as on the polished wood dance floor planked over the sandy lawn. She untangled her low heel from between two decorative rocks. She wasn't here to socialize tonight. She'd come to find little Nina's father.

If only she had a better idea of what he looked like.

Her longtime friend and old sorority sister—Nina's biological mother—had told Phoebe that Kyle Landis was the baby's daddy a couple of months ago when she'd asked for "just a little help" with Nina while she went on an audition for a dinner-theater production in Florida. Bianca had been so excited to get her prebaby body back, insisting this was her chance to provide a better life for her daughter.

Who could have known Bianca wouldn't return?

Phoebe hugged Nina closer, all the more determined to make sure this precious baby had a stable life. Which meant finding Kyle Landis, a man she'd never met in the flesh. She'd hoped to ID him by his Air Force uniform, but the place was packed with tall, dark-haired guys decked out in formal military gear. Medals gleamed in the moonlight.

Cupping the back of Nina's bonnet-covered head as the little one finally dozed off, Phoebe scanned the sea of faces, their profiles shadowy with only the illumination of moon, stars and pewter tiki torches. She only had an older photo to go by, a picture tucked deep in the bottom of the flowered diaper bag slung over her clean shoulder. No way was she going to disturb Nina by looking, not now that the baby was nearly out for the count.

He used to appear in the newspapers frequently when his late father had been a senator. Then his mother and brother had stepped into the political spotlight, too. But the family kept Kyle out of the media's scrutiny as much as possible for safety's sake because of his tours of duty in war zones.

The crush of people grew thicker, faces tougher to see. As much as she hated to draw attention to herself, she was going to have to ask for help finding—

"Can I get you something?"

The deep voice rumbled from behind her as if in answer to her very thoughts, jolting her with a clear shot of sexy bass on the salty ocean breeze. Lordy, the waiter must rack up tips with that bedroom voice of his. She glanced over her shoulder to ask for a napkin—she'd forgotten the burp rag again, damn it.

Her smile froze.

Captain Kyle Landis—in the flesh, all right.

His dark brown hair was trimmed military short, mellow blue eyes creased at the corners from a deep tan she knew he'd earned in a Middle Eastern desert. A broad forehead and strong jawline gave him a masculine appeal just shy of harsh.

She should have realized the guy would be even better looking in person. He was a lucky son of a gun from an established old Southern family—handsome and rich, with a smoky voice to boot. He'd even re-portedly survived a crash unscathed. His muscled chest in a blue uniform jacket sported at least double the medals of most here, perhaps only outdone by his stepfather, a general.

What were the odds of Kyle finding her tonight, instead of the other way around? But then, as the guest of honor, maybe he felt obligated to make sure everyone else was having a good time.

"Can I get you something?" he repeated, a cut-crystal whiskey glass cradled in his hand.

An older woman angled past, whipping a full, ruffled train against Phoebe's leg. The scent of strong perfume made Nina sneeze. She readjusted the baby, wishing they were at home in her bentwood rocker rather than here with this man. "I actually don't need help anymore, since I was looking for *you*."

A dimple dug into his cheek with his one-sided smile. "I'm sorry, if we've met before, I'm not remembering."

That dimple would have been charming if she hadn't already heard from Bianca to be wary of his prep-school-polished sense of humor. She might be out of her financial league here, but she was a smart, determined woman.

Phoebe forged ahead, needing to say something before he turned her over to a bouncer. "I'm not here for myself."

He glanced behind her quickly, then focused his full, deep-blue-eyed attention on her face again. "Which one of my pals are you with? We don't get many chances to meet the wives."

"I'm not married." But she had been. She shoved away even the thought of Roger before the inevitable stab of pain could steal her focus.

Kyle's gaze flicked briefly to Nina, then away. So much for him recognizing his child on sight.

To be fair, he didn't even know about Nina's existence. Bianca had insisted early in the pregnancy that, while she wasn't sure if she wanted to keep the baby, she would inform the baby's father. Then later said she'd chickened out, then couldn't find him and certainly didn't want to send this kind of news to him overseas through his family.

As if Bianca would've even gotten past personal assistants to talk to anyone in his famous family. It had been a major challenge to gate-crash this shindig, but no security could outdo her determination.

That drive—along with channeling some acting tips she'd picked up from Bianca—and Phoebe had convinced them all she was the caterer's assistant's wife. Easy enough to do, since she was more the friend-next-door than the flashy-leading-lady.

Nothing could stop her, not now that Kyle had come home. Somebody had to tell him about his new "little" responsibility and since Bianca was MIA, that left it up to her.

Might as well get this over with. "Is there somewhere we can step aside to talk?"

"I'm sorry, but my mother would haul me back in by my ear if I tried to duck out of my own welcome-home party." He angled closer, the fresh scent of his aftershave teasing her nose. "Maybe later, though?"

Undeniable interest flared in his cobalt-blue eyes, his full attention fixed on her.

Holy crap. Could he actually be hitting on her? She'd prepared herself for any possible reaction from him—except that.

She jolted back a step, holding up one hand. "Wait, that's not what I meant."

And even if he were interested enough to

actually contact her, what if it took him a week to call? She didn't have another week to waste waiting for him to phone her back.

Nina didn't have a week.

Phoebe patted between the baby's shoulders, praying she would stay asleep. The last thing she needed was a colicky nuclear meltdown. "I have to speak with you for five minutes out of earshot of everyone else. I promise I won't keep you long and you can get back to your welcome-home party. Perhaps you could just escort me to the door? Then you'll know I'm truly on my way out of your hair."

"Fair enough." He set his drink on the bar behind him. "Do you need some help with the kid?"

Instinctively, she backed farther away until her butt bumped a column plant-holder, jostling the fern on top.

Laughing, he held out both hands. "Hey, no need to freak out. I won't drop her. I've never been much of a kid person, but I'm getting practice lately with my nephew."

Nina had a cousin. How wild to think about, and imagine them playing together happily. Nina needed a life full of people who loved her. And the sooner Phoebe cleared this up, the sooner Nina would be settled. "We're fine, but thanks for asking. Just lead the way and we'll follow."

"Let me know if you change your mind."

He turned his broad shoulders sideways to slide past a pair of tuxedo-clad teens sneaking refills from the champagne fountain. Kyle plucked the glasses from their hands on his way by and passed them to a man from the catering staff.

He led Phoebe around a corner and stopped

in a small, empty alcove with a spindly iron bench and two more large potted ferns on Grecian-pillar stands. The party noise muffled down a notch, although the laughter of a nearby couple made her itchy for a room with a door to close. The nook just past an ivy-covered trellis wasn't totally private, but it would have to do.

Stepping away from his towering presence for a bit of breathing room, she eased the diaper bag down onto the iron bench and rolled the kink out of her shoulder. "Do you remember someone named Bianca Thompson?"

His eyes went from friendly to reserved. "Yes, why do you ask?"

Nearby laughter swelled as two trophy-wife types ducked into the alcove, one with a silver cigarette case in her hands and the other weaving tipsily behind her. "Oh," the woman said, tucking her cigarette case surreptitiously behind her back, "excuse me."

Kyle's easy smile came back. "No problem, ladies. I think there's another bench just past the palmetto tree wrapped in lights."

"Thank you, Captain." The woman flashed a smile back, "advertising" with a length of too-tanned leg through the gown's excessive slit.

Phoebe watched them disappear faster than the after-waft of their cologne. She turned back to Kyle. "You don't deny knowing Bianca?"

"This is getting strange here." He scratched the back of his neck. "You need to cut to the chase… What was your name again?"

"Phoebe—" She paused as a uniformed waiter tucked into the alcove, stopped short and then spun back around to leave, apparently looking for a place to ditch work undetected for a few seconds.

Good luck with that, buddy, because apparently there wasn't a quiet place to be found at this crammed-to-the-gills gala.

She hefted Nina's limp—and growing heavier by the second—body higher onto her shoulder. Her sweet weight and baby-shampoo-fresh scent tugged at her heart with a reminder of just how important this meeting was to both of their futures. "Phoebe. My name is Phoebe Slater. Bianca and I were sorority sisters, but we've stayed in touch over the years."

Although not as much as she would have liked during the past two months. She still could hardly believe Bianca would just drop off her baby daughter and not look back.

"Nice to meet you, Phoebe," he said, one eyebrow arching up with the implication his patience had about run dry.

Time was up. There wasn't ever going to be the perfect setting for this kind of revelation. She resisted the urge to clutch the baby tighter and bolt. This wasn't her child, but she loved her as dearly as if they shared the same blood. In fact, this would be her only chance at motherhood—however brief. When her husband she'd loved more than life had died, all hopes of being a mother had died with him.

No blue eyes would distract her from protecting Nina, no social brush-offs would dislodge her from her mission. She would do anything, *anything* to secure Nina's future.

Phoebe braced her shoulders and her resolve to push forward with her plan, even if it meant making a deal with a blue-eyed devil. "Meet Nina, your daughter."

* * *

Damn.

Another gold digger.

Party noise droning behind him like the buzz of aircraft engines, Kyle rocked back on his heels, his polished uniform shoes squeaking. He'd worked in intel during his Air Force career, but it didn't take an investigative mind to determine something was *way* off with this woman.

The second he'd seen Phoebe Slater sidle past security, he had been gut-slammed by her appeal. He still couldn't pull his eyes off her beacon-pale blond hair, clasped back simply, and her wide mouth that didn't need lipstick or collagen to make it kiss-me sexy.

The kid had given him a moment's pause, but his attention had shifted fast enough back to the totally hot female. He'd initially sized

her up as a down-to-earth sort with un-
adorned appeal, a simple but intriguing
woman. Not so simple after all, apparently.

Perhaps she wasn't a gold digger. Maybe
she was just a deluded psycho.

He tucked his fisted hands firmly behind
him, glad now he'd chosen a locale that was
only semiprivate, rather than totally secluded.
"Ma'am, I'm certain we've never met before
tonight, and I'm even more certain we've
never slept together." He would have definitely remembered her. "As cute as your kid
is, she's not mine."

Phoebe Slater visibly bristled, her choco-
late-brown eyes darkening. "She's not my
daughter. I'm just caring for her while her
mother—Bianca Thompson—is away at an
audition in Southern Florida. Bianca and I
went to school together before she started

pursuing her acting career, and I became a history professor. But that's all beside the point." Her throat moved in a long swallow. "I'm here because Nina needs her father. She's five months old now."

The hairs on the back of his neck prickled.

He *had* slept with Bianca Thompson, but he'd used protection—he always did. They hadn't known each other well. It had been more of an impulsive hookup on both their parts, over a year ago, before he'd left for a year-long deployment to Afghanistan.

Just about the right timing.

His gaze snapped to the kid blinking groggily at him with light blue eyes just like his mother, brothers... Damn. Plenty of people had blue eyes, and plenty of people knew what his family looked like. And those same people would know about the Landis family's hefty investment portfolio. His youngest brother had even had a false paternity suit filed against him by someone he'd actually cared about.

Kyle bit back a curse. He needed to stop this conversation now, until he could regroup with some more information on this woman. Preferably in a place where he didn't have to worry about everyone from the press to the governor of South Carolina overhearing.

"Ma'am—"

"Slater. I am Phoebe Slater." She rubbed soothing little circles between the baby's shoulders, swaying back and forth like a pro.

Impressive. He knew from his brother and sister-in-law how tough it was to keep a little rug rat quiet at this age.

"Okay, Ms. Slater, let's schedule a time for this conversation when we're not trying to speak over a band and we're certain not to be interrupted—"

"And this is Nina." She angled sideways so the baby's chubby-cheeked face was fully in view.

Cute kid. But that was irrelevant. "I don't think this is the—"

"Her mother is Bianca Thompson.

She'd said that already, but hearing it again made him really look at the baby. She didn't have Bianca's red hair. The baby had dark brown hair. Like him. "Where is Bianca? Why am I talking to you instead of her?"

His suspicions mounted as he tried to put the pieces together before this blew up in a very public setting. His mother had gone to a lot of trouble putting together this shindig commemorating his homecoming. It meant a lot to her, since this also marked the end of his military commitment. In two weeks, he would start his new career as the head of the Landis Foundation's international interests.

He didn't want his family upset needlessly by a scene. Family was everything.

His eyes flicked uneasily back to the baby, looking too darn cute in her pink dress.

"I was only supposed to watch Nina until Bianca settled in at her new place in Southern Florida. Then weeks turned into months. When she stopped calling, I got worried and notified the police to file a missing person's report. Which then brought child services into the picture, and if I don't figure out something soon—" Phoebe's chin quivered briefly before steadying again "—they're going to put Nina into the foster care system."

He wasn't sure what she was up to

anymore, but truth be told, even a conversation with a crazy woman was more engaging than the small talk he'd made tonight with people who were mostly here for the free food and a chance to rub elbows with politicians. Phoebe Slater was anything but boring.

"So you want me to take in this child, with no proof of who you are or who this kid is."

"Just hear me out." Her eyes turned a deeper shade of brown, panic glinting.

His instincts went on alert. If this woman was a crook—or a psycho—the kid could be in danger. That changed things entirely. "You know, maybe I should hold the baby after all, while we check into things."

"You're doubting me now, aren't you? Smart man."

She secured the sleeping baby and leaned to dig through the voluminous diaper bag on the bench. Good Lord, he could have stuffed all his military gear in that sack.

His eyes dropped to her hips, to the sweet curve of her bottom as she rifled past diapers and a bottle. Was she really a college professor? He'd certainly never had any profs that looked like her.

What a waste to have all that appeal packaged in a woman he couldn't go anywhere near. She straightened and turned back to face him, drawing his eyes upward.

"Okay, Captain Landis, I thought you would want proof. And well you should." She pulled out a file of papers. "I've got her birth certificate, photos and a notarized letter from Bianca stating I'm a babysitter for Nina, authorizing me to get medical attention for her. I even included a copy of my driver's license."

He took the file from her and flipped it open,

angling so his shoulders blocked any passersby from possibly seeing the contents. He scanned the first page, with pictures of Bianca Thompson holding a baby with wide blue eyes.

The hair on the back of his neck prickled again. He turned to the next page and read through the birth certificate…

With his name in the "father" box.

He exhaled hard. True or not, he still needed a second to process seeing his name in that context. Not that he had anything against kids—he liked his nephew well enough. He'd just planned to leave perpetuating the Landis name to his brothers.

Thumbing to the last page, he found a copy of Phoebe Slater's driver's license. The picture was unflattering, to say the least, with eyes deer-in-the-headlight wide and no smile, but without question it was her.

All of which proved nothing, in and of itself. Why the hell hadn't Bianca notified him? She had plenty of contact numbers. He may have been out of the country, but his family had all been firmly here on U.S. soil.

The more he thought about this, the less it made sense. *If* the little girl was his, he would move forward and take responsibility. Landises didn't shirk their responsibilities. But, for the child's safety as well, he needed to investigate this claim *and* this woman further.

He closed the file and tucked it under his arm. "I'm going to need some time to look over this. I can't just take home a child because you say—"

She laughed, her breath gusting a straggled strand of blond hair. She scraped it away and behind her ear. "No, you completely mis-understand. I don't want you to take her. I got the message loud and clear from Bianca that you're not interested in settling down. And truly, I love this little girl." She rested her cheek on top of the baby's head with unmistakable maternal affection. "I want to be her mother. I want to adopt her, if at all possible."

He should be relieved…but something was still off. His instincts from battling overseas bellowed loud and clear that there were more land mines ahead. "Then why are you here?"

"I'm here to keep Nina out of the foster care system," she said, her words tumbling together as she blurted, "I'm here to ask you to marry me."

Two

Phoebe bit her lip, cringing inside over having blurted the "proposal" rather than easing him into the idea the way she'd mentally rehearsed.

Too late to call back the words now. The band segued into a Motown ballad, the crooner's tune filling the silence while she waited for Kyle's reaction. Not for the first time, she cursed Bianca for disappearing, while praying that her old friend hadn't landed in some kind of trouble. Or worse.

Meanwhile, she had to make use of whatever allies she could find, and please, please she hoped Kyle would fall into that category. She searched his face for some clue of his feelings, but he guarded his emotions well.

Finally, he raised a hand shoulder-high.

She tensed, wondering, waiting and definitely keeping her trap shut for now. She was a thinker, a plotter, damn it. Bianca was the impulsive one.

Kyle spanned a broad palm along Nina's back protectively, his gold college ring glinting in the flickering candlelight. "Let me hold the kid for a minute."

Relief gusted from her so fully that she hadn't even realized she'd been holding her breath.

She'd hardly dared hope it would be this easy for him to connect with his daughter—

Then the glow from the pewter tiki torches revealed the glimmer of alarm in his eyes, quickly covered as he flashed a pacifying smile.

Damn.

He thought she was off her rocker to the point he feared for Nina. As if she would do anything to harm this child. Although she'd surely screwed up in pushing so hard and fast for his help.

"I'm not crazy, and I'm the last person who would ever hurt Nina." She cradled the sleeping girl closer until he relaxed his hands, if not his stance. "I didn't mean to spring that last part on you so bluntly, but you were ready to leave and I don't have time to be subtle."

"Is there a *subtle* way to ask a total stranger to marry you?"

Phoebe ignored his sarcasm. "Child services is going to take her since I can't find her mother. I just need to buy a little time until I can settle things for Nina."

She didn't know what else to do. Nina had no one except her… And this man. Her father.

"I still think you're half-cracked, but I'm listening." He folded his arms over his chest.

Was he settling in or blocking her exit? Either way, she needed to talk fast.

"Okay, so maybe the marriage idea seems extreme, but I'm desperate here." Backing off the proposal seemed prudent since she had a serious aversion to ending up in a straitjacket. "My primary concern is keeping Nina secure. She's already had too much upheaval, with Bianca dropping out of her life so abruptly."

"This is a lot to digest," he said, his voice neutral, his eyes still watching her guardedly.

His military aura swelled unmistakably. He might not be thinking of himself as Nina's father, but he clearly would stand between the baby girl and any perceived threat all the same.

Her frayed nerves snapped. "If you can think of another alternative to keeping her out of the foster care system, I'm more than happy to climb on board."

He cocked a thick, dark brow. "Excuse me for being slow on the uptake, but I didn't know until ninety seconds ago that I even had a child."

"If you'd stayed in touch with Bianca after you deployed, you may have—" She bit her tongue to keep from saying anything else, when she longed to shout out her frustration as she saw her last hope for help slipping away.

His eyebrows slammed down and together. "You can't actually be blaming me because

Bianca kept this a secret. If what you say is even true. I had my hands full fighting a war."

Her anger defused and sympathy slid into the void. "I'm sorry. You're right. This is a lot to take in and I don't mean to be combative."

His jaw flexed as he paused to gather his composure. "Arguing won't get us anywhere."

"I completely agree."

Still, he kept his post in front of the arbor trellis, sprawling ivy cascading down the sides like spiky tentacles ready to snag her in place. "Regardless of what came before, we need to decide on a plan of action from this point forward, which I absolutely refuse to talk about in a place where anyone could overhear. There are no less than seven people from the press attending this shindig my mother put together to welcome me back."

He had a point there. While press coverage

could be helpful in finding Bianca, it could also bring the wrath of child services down on her head. She had to strike a delicate balance here.

At least Kyle was still talking to her. Maybe he would have an idea, and if not, then she could bring up the marriage idea again with more finesse. It was outrageous, sure, but not that totally out there. She reassured herself for probably the thousandth time that this wasn't a totally crazy idea. Although she could imagine her long-dead parents wincing over her whole plan.

She'd thought this through. People got hitched in Vegas every day for far more flimsy reasons. Wedding vows meant next to nothing to most people these days.

And they would certainly mean nothing to her ever again.

She started toward him. Their cubby of space went darker as another person strode under the ivy-covered arch, snapping Phoebe back into the present. She needed to be on guard for those press people he'd mentioned. Backlit, the shadowy figure was still obviously a woman.

"Kyle, dear, there you are." An older blond woman stepped into the glow of the flickering light. She rested a hand on his arm, manicured nails tipped white.

His mother.

Even if Ginger Landis Renshaw weren't famous for her political prowess as a former senator and then secretary of state, Phoebe would have noticed the family resemblance. Their hair color was different but their faces, their smiles, were the same.

Somewhere in her early fifties and carrying

it well, Ginger smoothed a hand over her simple red Chanel evening gown, almost managing to disguise her curiosity. "Our guests are beginning to ask where you've run off to."

"Mom, we need to find an empty room and talk. Immediately." He stepped aside, clearing the view for the woman's gaze to fall squarely on Phoebe.

Ginger's blue eyes darkened from curiosity to concern. "Kyle? What's going on?"

"Not now, Mom," he said quietly, his voice urgent. "We need to move this to a room, preferably one with a closed door."

She straightened with a take-charge efficiency that had won respect around the world during her secretary-of-state days. That political sway continued now in her tenure as ambassador to a small but politically powerful

South-American country. "Of course. This way."

She tucked out of their garden nook and sliced a path straight into the country club. A quick flick of her hand had the manager rushing ahead to unlock his office. Phoebe followed, unable to squelch her awe at this woman who made things happen so effortlessly.

Damn it. Forget awe. She would stand down anyone for Nina if need be. But she hoped she would find an ally in a political powerhouse.

The door clicked closed behind them, sealing them inside an office with looming dark furniture and heavy tapestry upholstery. The scent of furniture polish and fresh-cut flowers coated the air thickly.

Ginger turned toward her son but looked at Phoebe and gestured toward a wingback chair. "Have a seat, dear. Even little babies can grow quite heavy when you've been holding them for too long."

Phoebe blinked back her surprise and sat. Disobeying this woman wouldn't dawn on her, and her feet were throbbing. All the same, she wouldn't relax her guard for even a second. Winning his mother's support was just as important as gaining Kyle's trust.

Ginger pinned her son with a questioning stare.

He scratched the back of his neck. "Mom, it appears I may have left a child behind when I went to Afghanistan."

Kyle knew one thing in this crazy, mixed-up night. Give a Landis a crisis and they start things cranking at Mach speed.

He had no more than announced the possibility of this child being his and his mom had spun into action. She'd called for her trusted assistant and gathered the rest of the family. So much for keeping things secret.

With four Landis brothers, two of whom were married, that made for quite a group packed into the country club office. His brother Sebastian sat at the sprawling wood desk, putting his legal eagle-eye and degree to work reviewing the documents. The rest of the family seemed transfixed around the wingback chair where Phoebe fed the little scrap of a kid a bottle. Kyle paced. He damn near wore a hole in the Persian rug as he moved restlessly behind his brother. Sebastian was a year younger than Kyle, but his quiet soberness had always made him seem older. They needed his calm efficiency right now.

Sebastian closed the file and glanced up somberly. "Is she your daughter?"

Kyle stopped in his tracks and dropped to sit on the edge of the desk, his foot twitching. "It's a distinct possibility." A possibility that still sucker-punched him harder than the missile that had taken down his aircraft in Afghanistan. He pinched the bridge of his nose briefly before his hand fell away. "If she's really Bianca Thompson's daughter, the timing of our, uh, week together lines up."

"A week, huh?" A rare hint of humor lit his normally serious brother's eyes.

Kyle wasn't in the mood to laugh. "We hooked up when I was in between rotations overseas. Neither of us was interested in anything long-term."

"You never are." Sebastian looked away and back at the papers.

Yeah, he wasn't known for serious relationships, but at least he understood himself, rather than sending out mixed signals. "Which makes it all the more ironic that Phoebe would toss out a marriage proposal to me."

"I think it makes her seem like a more logical type." Sebastian kept his voice low enough that the cluster of people a few feet away wouldn't hear. "If she knows your reputation, then she has no reason to worry about you growing attached to her or the baby."

"She said she only tossed it out there in desperation. That she didn't really mean it, and could I come up with something else." Still it rattled around in his head. "You got any suggestions?"

Sebastian scrubbed a hand over his face, a near mirror image of Kyle's. "I think the first order of business is finding out if she's really yours. I've never been one who could see

Great-aunt Whoever's chin on some infant, but I have to confess, she looks just like a Landis."

The uncertainty was already chewing him up inside. "Any idea how long it takes for the results of a paternity test?"

"Gotta admit, I've never needed one." His eyes slid over to his wife with obvious affection. Their son had been born a few months ago, a surprise pregnancy after the crushing loss of the baby daughter they'd adopted, only to have the birth mother change her mind. "Jonah should know, though."

Their youngest brother had always been a hell-raiser, so much so that after a while it became tough to distinguish between truth and reputation. Kyle had always understood his younger brother better than the rest of the family, although the military had helped him rein in his wilder impulses.

And yet still, somehow, he may have screwed up. "The sooner we can clear this up, the better."

"What do you know about her?" Sebastian nodded toward Phoebe, who was lifting the baby up to burp, a hand towel from the bathroom draped over her shoulder.

"Nothing at all." Kyle flipped open the manila file folder again and thumbed through the papers. "I'd never met her, but those photos of her with Bianca look real."

"The private investigator I keep on retainer will be able to verify her story by morning. The fact that she lives and works in state makes things easier all the way around." Sebastian tapped the documents spilling out across the desk. "Everything seems authentic and in order though. We'll see soon."

Not soon cnough. "So, we're stuck for

now." Kyle lowered his voice, even though no one across the room seemed to be paying any attention to them. "Either she's on the up-and-up helping out a friend, in which case she needs help, so the baby stays. Or she's a nutcase, in which case for the baby's safety, she has to stay."

"Be careful, my brother." Sebastian leaned closer. "There's a lot of money at stake here."

Sebastian's wife glanced over her shoulder. "Men are so cynical."

Damn, he could have sworn they were keeping their voices down. Could Phoebe have overheard them too? Not that they'd really said anything that mattered. She should expect they would have her investigated.

The wife of their oldest brother, Matthew, stepped aside, opening the circle as she caressed the slight curve of her stomach.

"They're right to be concerned," Ashley said. "I've seen some sad cases of how heartless people can be when it comes to the needs of a child."

Their youngest brother, Jonah, snorted, lounging on the other wingback chair, one leg draped over the armrest. "Who are you condemning here? The baby's mother or Phoebe?"

Ginger rested a hand on the back of Phoebe's chair and shot her sons a censuring stare that hadn't lost its impact over the years. "I'm sorry you had to hear that. My boys should be more diplomatic."

Kyle watched his mother win over Phoebe with a few well-chosen words. There was no doubting who wore the diplomatic mantle in their family.

"I'm not offended," Phoebe said. "In fact, I'm relieved that you're all being practical about this. That bodes well for Nina, and I have nothing to hide."

Jonah twitched back an overlong lock of hair from his brow. "Lady, I have to confess, this all sounds a little hinky to me. You wouldn't be the first person to want a piece of the Landis lucrative pie."

"I'm not here for money." She patted Nina's back steadily until the baby burped, then lowered her to the crook of her arm. "I only need time. I want to keep her out of foster care until we can find her mother, and if we can't, then it's my hope I can adopt her."

Jonah tugged his dangling tux tie free…not that it had even been tied before they stepped back here for the family confab with Phoebe. "Then let the legal system sort it out. If you're best for her, that's where she'll land."

Ginger waved her rebellious youngest son

up from the chair and motioned for pregnant Ashley to sit.

Ashley smiled her appreciation as she sat with a heavy sigh. "It's not that cut-and-dried. I was lucky."

Phoebe smoothed her hand over the baby's head with obvious affection, but her face creased with concern. "Yours is a success story, then?"

"My foster sisters and I found a wonderful home with 'Aunt' Libby and were better off. Claire's biological mother wanted to keep her, but was too young and didn't have the money. Starr's parents were criminals who refused to relinquish custody. My parents gave me up." Quiet Ashley grew more fervent as she spoke. "Not all of the girls who were placed with Aunt Libby came straight there from their biological parents, though. Most foster parents are well-meaning, big-hearted people, but there are some…" She shook her head in obvious disgust.

The defender in Kyle, the military part of him that had spent the past six years of his life protecting, made him want to pluck the kid up and keep her safe from the world.

How much stronger would those feelings become if it turned out the baby was his?

Phoebe rested her cheek on Nina's head. "I don't want to run any risk of Nina landing in an unloving home for even a day."

"Exactly," Ashley agreed. "Some people don't have choices. There are options here for little Nina."

His mother nodded. "I've already spoken with my assistant and she's scheduled a paternity test."

"On a weekend?"

Apparently Phoebe didn't grasp his mother's ability to move mountains.

Ginger toyed with one of her diamond stud earrings. "We'll have an answer before child services opens on Monday morning."

Time to test how far she was willing to go with this. He put his hands behind his back, military bearing tough to shake even with his separation papers in the works. "Since you all seem so certain Nina is mine, we might as well start moving her things into my wing of the house."

"Excuse me?" Phoebe's eyes went wide with alarm. "Um, Nina and I are already settled in our hotel, but thank you."

Kyle braced a hand across the door. "If there's even a chance that's my daughter, I'm not letting you just walk out of here with her."

Phoebe looked around nervously, then bolstered, her arms locked around Nina. "I'm not leaving her behind."

"I don't expect you to." *Nobody* was going anywhere until he had answers. "You'll both be staying with me at the family compound."

Three

She didn't have a choice but to go with him, and she knew it. Sitting in the back of Kyle's Mercedes sedan beside Nina in her car seat, Phoebe just wished she'd foreseen this twist in the plans.

His broad shoulders, encased in the uniform jacket, spread in front of her in the driver's seat. He guided the luxury car through the security gate into the Landis family beach compound. As the gates swung closed behind them, she shifted closer to Nina, the infant asleep and drooling in her rear-facing car seat. Morning was going to come early after this late night and she needed any edge she could scavenge to soothe her already frazzled nerves.

By appealing to Kyle for help, she'd also made herself vulnerable. One call from him to child services could steal her few days' window to secure Nina's future. She hadn't felt so powerless since she'd watched helplessly while her husband had drowned.

Her gaze skimmed nervously ahead to the beachside Hilton Head mansion owned by the Landis family. Kyle had told her that his lawyer-brother and wife had a home a few miles away, and the oldest brother, a senator, and his wife had an antebellum mansion in downtown Charleston. Kyle had kept his gear in the third-floor quarters of the mansion since he'd deployed so often.

She'd rubbed elbows with plenty of affluent families at the college fund-raisers, but she'd never visited anywhere nearly this opulent. In spite of insisting she didn't need money, a hotel over the weekend would have taken a chunk out of her account. She had to keep her savings intact for any legal fees she might need in adopting Nina. Staying here was the fiscally smart thing to do.

She'd seen photos from a *Good Housekeeping* spread when she'd looked up the Landis family on Google for more details, and she'd read about their diversified fortune that increased under the savvy care of each generation. But no picture could have prepared her for the breathtaking view. On prime oceanfront property, they'd built a sprawling white three-story house with Victorian peaks overlooking the Atlantic. A lengthy set of stairs stretched upward to the second-story wraparound porch that housed the main entrance.

Latticework shielded most of the first floor, which appeared to be a large entertainment area. Just as in Charleston, many homes so close to the water were built up as a safeguard against tidal floods from hurricanes.

The attached garage had so many doors she stopped counting. His sedan rolled to a stop beside the house, providing a view of the dense green bushes behind them and the Atlantic shore in front of them. An organic-shaped pool was situated between the house and beach, the chlorinated waters of the hot tub at the base churning a glistening swirl in the moonlight.

He put the car in Park and reached for the door. "I'll get your things from the trunk while you unload the munchkin."

Kyle stepped out before she could even answer. Apparently he'd inherited his mother's take-charge attitude. Phoebe walked around to the other side of the Mercedes, security lights activating like sunrise coming early, and unhooked the carrier from the car-seat base so as not to wake Nina.

He lifted her small suitcase and duffel with a porta-crib out of the trunk. "You sure do travel light compared to most women I've met."

"I had only planned to stay overnight." She'd pretty much counted on getting his support and then heading home in the morning, a naïve fantasy now that she saw how complicated things were becoming as reality played out. "I have a job to get back to in Columbia."

He gestured toward the sprawling staircase. "Then you can leave Nina here."

She hesitated at the bottom step, suddenly claustrophobic about entering his house. Sheesh, it wasn't like he could lock them away in the attic. "I won't abandon her."

"And neither will I," he said with unmistakable determination, which made her glad for Nina.

If she could trust him.

She looked away from his persuasive blue eyes and back up the length of stairs. This would be temporary, until he left on his next assignment, then she could resume her life. "It seems we're at an impasse."

"What about your job?" His intoxicating bass drifted after her shoulder as he followed her up the outside wooden steps.

"I'm teaching all my classes online this

semester anyway." She'd adjusted her schedule to be with Nina, seeing this as her once-in-a-lifetime chance to take care of a baby. Little had she known when Bianca dropped off her daughter… "I can work from here until we have things settled."

Until he left.

She would have her life back on track shortly. His job, along with his track record for short relationships, would have him out of her life soon. And she really didn't have any other options if she wanted to keep Nina.

She pointed to the cluster of live oaks and palmettos framing a two-story carriage house. "Who lives there?"

"My youngest brother, Jonah. He's finishing up his graduate studies in architecture. He stays here between internship trips to Europe."

White with slate-blue shutters, the carriage

house was larger than most family homes, certainly bigger than her little apartment in downtown Columbia. "It's lovely."

She understood he came from money, but seeing Kyle's lifestyle laid out so grandly only emphasized their different roots. Phoebe gripped the increasingly heavy car seat with both hands as she reached the top of the stairs. The tall double doors opened before Kyle could even reach forward.

His lawyer brother, Sebastian, filled the entrance, their appearances close enough to be mistaken for twins. Except the lawyer didn't have Kyle's laugh lines. "You finally made it."

Kyle deposited her bags on the polished wood floor. "I drove slower because of the kid. Where's Mom?"

"Still at the club with the general closing out the party so it's not as obvious we're gone." Sebastian eyed Phoebe and Nina briefly then looked back at his brother. "We need to talk."

Kyle ushered her into the cavernous foyer. "As soon as I get them settled."

A woman, the wife of the lawyer brother, stood waiting in the archway leading to a mammoth living room with a wall of windows overlooking the ocean. "I can show her around." The woman—Marianna, she'd been called back at the country club—swept a loose dark curl from her face. "You'll want to put the baby to bed. I'll take you to your rooms."

Phoebe glanced into the hall where Kyle had deposited her bag. "Did the porta-crib make it inside?"

"Don't worry," Marianna reassured her. "Everything's taken care of."

Still, Phoebe hesitated. What did the brothers

need to speak about that she couldn't hear? Suspicion nipped her ragged nerves, but there wasn't anything she could do about it, especially in her exhausted state. Maybe she could ferret some information of her own from this woman while Kyle was out of the room.

She smiled back at Marianna. "Thank you, I appreciate your help."

Marianna extended her hand for the diaper bag. "Let me. Those things weigh a ton. Come on and I'll show you to the nursery."

"There's a nursery here?"

"My husband and I live a few miles away, but Grandma Ginger keeps everything we need here if our little guy needs to nap. Ginger's second husband, Hank Renshaw, also has grandchildren from his daughters. Between us all, we make good use of that room. You'll find everything you could possibly need in there."

Still, Phoebe hesitated. Giving Nina a room here, even a temporary one, seemed such a huge step. One she should have been happy about.

Marianna hitched the pink-flowered diaper bag over her shoulder. "There's a nursery monitor so you can hear the least little peep if she needs you."

Even swaying with exhaustion, Phoebe hesitated. "I don't think I could leave her to wake up alone in a strange place."

Marianna's face softened with understanding. "There's also a daybed in the nursery if you would rather sleep in there with her."

"Show me the way."

Marianna started the winding walk through pale-yellow halls until Phoebe wondered if she would be able to find her way back out of the Landis world again. Beach landscapes mingled with framed family candids that added a surprise touch of hominess to the designer decor. A grandfather clock ticked, their footsteps muffled by the light patterned Oriental rugs.

Phoebe couldn't take the silence any longer. Besides, she would never learn anything from the woman this way. "Aren't you going to ask me if I'm lying? Everyone else doubts me."

Marianna glanced back with a reassuring smile, her thick dark hair swishing like the clock's pendulum. "I believe you're telling us the truth about Nina being Kyle's daughter."

"How can you be so certain?"

Marianna gestured to a portrait on the hall wall, a painting of an infant boy. Undisguised love shone in her eyes. "That's my son, Sebastian Edward Landis Junior. And very obviously

Nina's cousin." She tapped four other framed images of babies along the way, all with striking blue eyes. "These are of Matthew, Kyle, Sebastian and Jonah when they were little. There's no mistaking the Landis look."

She totally agreed. The deep blue eyes, the signature one-sided smile…they all had it, as did Nina. "If you see the likeness, why can't they?"

"Because I'm evaluating with maternal eyes, and so are you." Marianna stopped in front of a closed door, her hand resting on the brass handle. "We see them in a way nobody else ever will."

Marianna's words stabbed her with an inescapable reality. "I'm not her mother."

"You're willing to do anything for Nina. In my eyes, that makes you her mother." Marianna looked at her with an understanding. "The family will want a paternity test for legal reasons, of course. They're that way about details, but truly it will protect Nina's interests as much as their own."

"Those results take a while, don't they?" Would they know soon enough to satisfy a family court judge?

"Nothing takes long when you're a Landis. They're an impatient bunch and have the money on hand to see that their wishes are met speedily. Don't worry. You'll get your answer quickly."

Marianna swept open the door to reveal an airy nursery, decorated in neutral sea-foam-green, a white crib on one wall with a coordinated white daybed tucked under a window. A fat, delicious-looking rocker and ottoman took up a corner underneath a mural of fairy-tale characters. "Here we are."

"Thank you for showing me the way." Phoebe stepped inside with mixed feelings, wishing she could have given Nina all this and more.

Marianna kept her hand on the open door. "I'm sure Kyle will check in when he's done talking with Sebastian, but I really need to head home now so the sitter can leave. I don't like being away from little Edward too long. Good luck."

"Hopefully I won't need it."

With a smile and a quick squeeze of her arm, Marianna seemed to sense her worry. "It will be fine. You'll both be fine. You'll see."

She closed the door behind her. The click reminded Phoebe of her plans to learn more from the woman. She hadn't found out much more than confirmation of what she'd already known in her heart. Nina was a Landis.

Long after Marianna left and Nina was

tucked in her crib, Phoebe sat on the daybed, hugging her knees and staring out at the ocean, unable to sleep. Too many questions, uncertainties, fears churned in her mind like the curling waves, rolling and retreating only to crash right back over her again. One thing shone through as clearly as the moonlight slashing away at the murky depths.

The Landises had power.

The kind of money and impatience that could buy an overnight paternity test could surely oust anyone who didn't belong in their elite world. With no blood claim to Nina, and Bianca gone, Phoebe could easily find herself at odds with Kyle all too soon.

After having been helpless while she'd watched her husband leave her, she couldn't tamp down the reflexive fear of having someone she loved taken from her again.

* * *

Parked behind the desk in the family study, Kyle scrubbed a hand along his bristly face that had long ago gone past a five-o'clock shadow. Early morning rays from the sun were just beginning to poke through the horizon and past floor-to-ceiling windows. Answers were piercing through just as surely.

Sebastian slept on the butter-yellow leather sofa in front of built-in library shelves of warm oak, but Kyle kept watch for the updates that had been coming in from the private investigator over his BlackBerry throughout the night, while doing some checking on his own. Money and the Internet provided a wealth of fast information.

So far, everything about Phoebe Slater's story checked out. She did, in fact, work at the University of South Carolina. She'd been a history professor on campus for three years, but for the fall semester had abruptly shifted to teaching only online classes—right about the time Nina would have entered her life full-time.

Bianca Thompson had indeed gone to school with Phoebe, and Bianca had given birth to a daughter named Nina.

He cradled his BlackBerry in his hand, staring at the latest report. The one that had surprised him.

Phoebe was a widow.

The circumstances of how her husband had died were simply listed as accidental drowning. That explained the haunted look that never left her eyes, even when she smiled, which was only when she looked at the kid.

This was getting complicated.

He shoved restlessly to his feet, pacing,

farther and farther away from the desk until he found himself making his way through the halls, toward the nursery where Marianna had said both Nina and Phoebe were staying. The door was cracked slightly open. The baby slept on in the crib his mother had set up for her grandchildren. They'd expected Matthew and Ashley's baby, due this winter, to be the next addition.

Who could have foreseen this?

He stepped deeper into the room—and stopped short.

Phoebe sat curled up in a corner of the daybed, asleep with her cheek resting against the windowsill. The sheet and coverlet twisted around her, attesting to a restless night. She still wore her little black number from the party, but she'd kicked off her strappy heels. The delicate arches of her bare feet called to him to stroke up her legs, explore the softness of her skin.

Her white-blond hair streaked over her face, the silver clasp discarded on the bedside table. Given they both wore the same clothes from the night before, they could have been a couple ending a long, satisfying night together.

Except she wasn't here for him. He started to back out and his uniform shoe squeaked.

Phoebe jolted awake. She shoved her silky blond hair away from her eyes, blinking fast, adding to her sultry morning-after appeal. "What? Nina?"

Kyle held a finger to his mouth. "The kid's still sleeping," he said softly, striding closer. "No need to get up yet, unless you want to go to shower and change." He really didn't need an image of her showering seared in his brain. "I can, uh, keep an eye on her."

He had his BlackBerry. He could still work from here.

She tugged a strap back up her arm. "I only meant to close my eyes for a second after I put on her pj's, and then I was going to unpack and put on something else. I must have fallen asleep."

"You have reason to be tired after yesterday, traveling with a baby on your own, then sleeping sitting up."

She shifted free of the tangled covers. "I didn't want her to wake up in a strange place and be scared."

An image of the little tyke's face scrunched up and crying sucker-punched him. Damn. And he didn't even know if she was his yet. "I really, uh, don't mind staying here with the kid while you sleep or shower."

"Her name is Nina."

"I know."

"You keep calling her 'the kid' or 'rug rat' or other generic things." Phoebe swung her slim legs from the bed, her simple black dress rucking up to her knees. "She's a person— Nina Elizabeth Thompson."

"I know what her name is." He dragged his eyes away from the enticing curve of Phoebe's legs and back to her equally intriguing face. "I saw her birth certificate. She's Nina."

Nina. A person. His eyes went to the crib where the little girl—*Nina*—slept on her back in fuzzy pink, footed pj's, sucking on one tiny fist in her sleep. A plastic panda teething toy lay beside her head.

For the first time in a crazy-ass night, he stood still long enough to think beyond the weekend. What if Nina turned out to be his? What if—as Sebastian had warned him—the courts still opted to put her in a foster home for even a short period of time? No. Freaking. Way. He had to stack the odds in his favor, in Nina's favor, just in case this little girl belonged to him.

Damn. He was actually considering Phoebe's proposal.

His hand fell to rest on the crib railing. He glanced over his shoulder at Phoebe. "You've given this paper marriage thing some thought."

"I haven't thought of much but that." She stood, her eyes wary. "Does this mean you're thinking about it, too?"

"I won't turn my back on my responsibility." He gripped the railing tighter. "We still have to wait for the paternity test. If she's not mine, marrying me won't help you. Bianca could have lied to you."

"She didn't." Phoebe crossed to stand

beside him and rested a hand on top of his. She squeezed his fingers lightly. "Nina is yours. I know it."

Her touch sent a jolt through him, just a simple touch, for Pete's sake. But her soft skin and light vanilla scent along with the pooling gratitude in her eyes had him downright itchy. He needed distance. Fast.

He stared at her hand pointedly and scrounged up some sarcasm. "I don't want you to do something stupid like fall in love."

She jerked her hand away and shook it as if it burned. "With you?"

"Who else have you asked to marry you?"

She laughed, then laughed again until her giggles tripped on a snort. The baby stirred and Phoebe went silent in a flash. He gripped her elbow and guided her back out into the hall, the doorway to the nursery still open.

She sagged against a wall alongside framed portraits of generations of baby Landises. "Don't worry." She gasped through a final laugh. "There's not a chance in hell I'll fall in love with you, but thanks for helping to lighten the mood for me."

What he'd meant as sarcastically funny suddenly didn't seem quite so humorous. "You're quite a buster there."

"I feel certain your, uh, man parts and ego will survive any potential busting."

"You seem mighty confident," he pressed, not even sure why, since she appeared so damned confident in her ability to keep her distance. "We've barely met. What have I done to make you dislike me so much? Not to sound egotistical, but I happen to have a lot of money. I've been told I have a pretty decent sense of humor, and I haven't noticed my face scaring off small children or animals."

"Other than the money part, the same could be said of me," she pointed out logically. "So since you already have plenty of money and don't need more from a wife, should I worry about you falling in love with me?"

Damn. She was good.

He couldn't stop a begrudging smile of respect at how she'd taken him down a notch. "Touché."

"I'll take that as a no."

"It's nothing personal. You're a beautiful, smart woman." A hot, sharp woman, a distinction that was even more pulse throbbing.

"Of course. Just as it wasn't personal when I laughed at you."

"Point well taken. I'm years away from being ready to settle down." He had his hands full launching his new life and career outside the military. "What about you?"

"I was married before."

He knew that already, of course, but letting on would make it clear he was already having her investigated. "Nasty divorce, huh?"

Her face went devoid of emotion, completely. He'd seen the look before on shell-shocked soldiers, numbing themselves for fear even the smallest emotion would shatter them to bits.

"He died," she said simply. "There's no room in my heart to love anyone else, not when he still fills every corner."

He exhaled hard. He knew that kind of love existed. He'd seen it with his parents, and again when his widowed mom remarried. He'd also seen how torn up his dad was over having to divide himself between career ambition and family. "Wow, that's hefty stuff there. I'm really sorry. How did he die?"

And why did he need to know more about it?

She looked down, staying silent.

Damn it, he needed to know everything about her. He had a short time to make an important choice, a majorly life-altering choice. He was used to making snap decisions in war, but he did so with as much intel as possible at his disposal. This shouldn't be any different. It wasn't personal.

"Phoebe, if we're going to get married, I should know. It will seem strange if someone thinks to ask and I don't have the right answer. For Nina's sake, we would need to make it look real."

"He drowned." A flash of undiluted grief bolted through her brown eyes like a lethal lightning strike. Then her face went blank again. She pushed away from the wall, away from him. "I should get back to Nina."

She spun on her heel, giving Kyle her back. She couldn't have been any clearer. Discussion over. Stand down. But he had his answer. That flash of grief in her eyes, followed by her abrupt shutdown left him with no doubts about where she stood on the subject of her ex-husband.

She was completely committed to another man.

That should have made the possibility of a paper marriage easier to contemplate, but damn, what a tangled mess. The door clicked closed behind her, and he reminded himself to take things one step at a time. First, he had to give a blood sample later today and wait for the paternity test results.

Although his instincts now shouted loud and clear that Phoebe Slater was telling the truth.

Four

"**M**arry me."

Kyle's demand—not request—bounced around inside Phoebe's head hot on the heels of the preliminary paternity results. Overwhelmed, she sagged in the front seat of his Mercedes, Nina asleep in the back after the exhausting day at the doctor's.

Butter-soft leather cradled her in luxury but offered little comfort for the stress knotting her neck. "Are you sure this is what you want to do?"

"Now's not the time to lose courage." He turned on the engine and adjusted the climate control for the muggy fall afternoon, all efficiency with a calm she envied. "I've talked it over with Sebastian and you were right about this being the fastest, most efficient way to secure Nina's future."

She stared through the windshield at the busy hospital complex parking lot. Her eyes were magnetically drawn to mothers with their children.

Mothers *and* fathers, too. "How long?"

"We'll get married on Monday— tomorrow." His jaw flexed with the first signs of stress.

A closer look revealed the pale hint under his tan.

She fisted her hands to keep from touching him, comforting him. She understood well how overwhelming this could all be, becoming a parent out of the blue. "No, I mean, how long would we keep up this charade? Who will we tell?"

"My family already knows what's going on. But beyond them, we would need to keep up appearances for Nina's sake."

"Appearances?" Holy crap, she'd meant fake marriage. Not pretend-to-be-real fake marriage.

"We'll need to live together, at least for a while." A slight grin eased the deep lines around his mouth. "But since I live at the Landis compound, we'll be surrounded by family to protect you from your lecherous husband."

She tucked her tongue in the side of her

mouth to keep from laughing, but she couldn't keep from smiling…until she thought about the next hurdle she should have considered before moving forward with this half-baked plan of hers. "What will your family think?"

More importantly, how would they react to her and Nina in their lives full-time? Her smile faded.

"You'll be welcomed as a Landis. And my mother will adore you simply because you love her…uh…granddaughter."

"That's a relief, at least." Nina would never be alone and abandoned again. "I wouldn't want things to be awkward when I bring Nina to visit."

"Visit?" He cocked a dark eyebrow and put the car in Reverse. "You'll need to stay at the house for at least a couple of months. At that point we could maintain two residences and claim work conflicts."

"Months?" She pressed a hand to her forehead.

He nodded curtly. "Long enough to get official custody worked out. Or until Bianca returns." His fist tightened on the gearshift. "If we don't hear from her, we can start divorce proceedings after a year."

"And about Nina?"

"I'll want visitation for me and for my family."

"Of course." She went weak with relief as he backed the car out of the parking spot. It must have been hard for him to concede full custody. Even though he hadn't known his daughter long, Phoebe had been around the Landises enough to recognize they took the notion of family loyalty to a whole new level.

Thank heavens, he wasn't going to fight her over custody. Tears burned behind her eyes and she blinked fast to hold them back, along with the urge to throw her arms around him in gratitude.

He was far too foreboding at the moment for a hug, his normal grin and lightheartedness nowhere in sight. Maybe he needed some reassurance, too. "I want to sign a prenup that makes it clear I have no claim to any Landis assets. Can your brother draw one up right away?"

"Except I will provide for Nina."

"Whatever you think is fair. I'm just so relieved you're not going to take her away."

"It's obvious from everything I've seen and learned about you that you've got her best interests at heart." He put the car in first gear, focusing his attention in front, his jaw flexing again, faster. "I'm in no position to be a full-time father with the travel load that comes with my job."

"Of course, that's totally understandable." Although she would have given up any job for Nina, had in fact made major concessions in her own work world. But she wasn't going to argue with him.

She did, however, want to ask him how he felt about all of this. Wasn't he frustrated over marrying a woman he barely knew? How did he feel about having a daughter, for crying out loud?

His resolute face shut her out as he steered onto the road. He was doing what needed to be done, fulfilling obligations. She should have been relieved over his emotional detachment.

Instead, she just felt hollow inside. "I need

it to be indisputably clear I'm only interested in Nina's well-being."

"Okay, then. I'll let Sebastian know so he can draw up the papers."

So cold and businesslike. Nothing in the arrangement resembled her emotional engagement to Roger. He'd proposed at the beach, no ring, no money, no complicated legal dealings to wade through. Just simple declarations of how much they loved each other and wanted to spend the rest of their lives together.

Yet, tomorrow she would be married to the man next to her. She'd gotten her way. Nina would be as safe as she could possibly arrange.

So why did a year suddenly sound like forever?

"By the power vested in me by the State of South Carolina, I now pronounce you husband and wife."

The jowly justice of the peace's proclamation resonated hollowly in Phoebe's ears, as if she was watching some kind of drama, far removed from her place beside Kyle. He wore a uniform again, a less formal version this time, but still with a jacket and tie for their courthouse wedding.

Everything had felt surreal since they'd rushed through the paternity test over the weekend, verifying what she'd known in her heart for certain since laying eyes on Kyle Landis. *He was Nina's biological father.*

Once Kyle had heard the paternity test results confirming she was his, he hadn't hesitated. Things had taken off at warp speed from there as he arranged for a Monday-afternoon wedding and an appointment with a family court judge shortly thereafter. The building complex made for one-stop shopping. This military man sure knew how to take command and move mountains.

Her fingers clutched around the bouquet of mango calla lilies with yellow roses. One of his sentimental sisters-in-law had thrust it into her hands—Ashley, the pregnant one married to the oldest politician brother. The other wife, Marianna, jostled her son on her hip, while Ginger stood beside her general husband and proudly held her new granddaughter, Nina.

Phoebe was a part of this family now, even if in name only.

The justice of the peace closed his folder containing the vows, a South Carolina flag and American flag behind him. "You may kiss the bride."

Phoebe looked up sharply at Kyle, any feeling of being a distant observer gone in a snap. Surely nobody expected them to go through with that part of the ceremony. Except the magistrate.

Kyle's face creased in a one-sided smile and he dipped his head toward her. She barely had time to register his oldest brother smothering a laugh before Kyle's mouth touched hers. Firm and gentle all at once, he kissed her. Her eyes closed, her ears roared and she lost track of everyone around her.

It had been so long since she'd felt a man's lips against hers. *Too* long. All her buried sensuality smoked back to life, steaming through her at just a simple, closed-lips caress. She wanted to open for more, more of this, more of him. Dots sparked in front of her eyes and she realized she'd forgotten to breathe.

He eased away slowly, thank goodness, so she had time to regain her balance. She clutched her bouquet, the floral scent teasing her with romanticism, and she opened her eyes. Kyle stared back at her for just an instant and then offered his elbow along with his typical lighthearted grin. She couldn't help smiling in return. Maybe, just maybe they could wade through this tangled mess.

As they turned toward the gathered family, Ginger held Nina out for them to hold. Kyle hesitated. Only for a second but long enough to bring her back to reality.

Phoebe thrust her bouquet of roses and lilies toward him and took the baby from Ginger. "Come here, sweetie. You were so good, so quiet."

She smoothed Nina's floral pinafore, adjusting the bonnet and booties until it seemed the momentary awkwardness had passed. But she hadn't forgotten. In spite of his speed in stepping up to the plate—honorable though that was—she could see he hadn't connected with Nina in any real way.

Not exactly the dream wedding day she'd fantasized about as a child, although she did feel like she was playing dress-up. She wore a knee-length gown borrowed from her new sister-in-law. The woman had graciously offered for Phoebe to keep the simple drape of pale yellow—with a Versace label. Marianna had insisted it didn't fit her anymore since she'd given birth to her son.

Nina grasped the strand of pearls resting on Phoebe's collarbone, Roger's gift to her the day they'd exchanged vows. Their wedding had been a simple affair, as well, but she hadn't minded. There'd been so little money in those days. He'd sold one of his first-edition books to pay for the necklace.

A fresh ache stabbed through her over the thought of never having Roger's baby. Nina was her one chance at motherhood, for however long that lasted.

A camera flash went off from a corner of the room, taken by a photographer hired by the Landises and soon to be released to the press. She blinked against the continuous barrage of flashes. At least the pictures had been staged by them, along with a story stating simply that Kyle had married his daughter's guardian.

She'd never seen such choreographed control before.

Kyle angled down conspiratorially. "Welcome to living with a family full of politicians. Watch what you say, and don't ever, ever chew with your mouth open. Well, unless you want it plastered on some Internet blog before you've swallowed your food."

Nina reached to pat his face, more of a thumping actually with her drool-covered palm, then she giggled and stuffed her plastic panda teething toy into her mouth. He was so charming with adults, why did he freeze with Nina? Or was it all children?

Regardless, he would be jetting off again soon to his base for some mission and she would be alone again with Nina. She just had to make it through a few days, not much time to ache for another kiss.

Ginger gave her a one-armed hug that seemed genuine and not just for the photo op. "Welcome to the family, dear."

"Thank you." Phoebe paused, lowering her voice. "But you know this is only temporary."

Her new mother-in-law gave her shoulder a final squeeze. "You're a Landis and you're an important part of my granddaughter's life. We'll worry about tomorrow when it gets here."

Panic constricted her breathing and the diamond-studded band on her finger seemed suddenly too tight. She should be happy. Everything was going just as Kyle had said it would, with his family accepting her even knowing the full circumstances.

Once the photographer had been ushered out, Marianna stepped alongside her with a supportive smile. "You look exhausted. Let's finish up the paperwork so you can get out of those heels."

If she could just go back to her apartment for even a little while and regroup. "You're so thoughtful to have loaned me your clothes, but I can't keep borrowing from you forever. I'll need to go back to Columbia. Nina and I are out of—"

Ginger waved a manicured hand. "No worries, dear. I've already taken care of everything. There are clothes waiting for you at the house. You can choose whatever you like. Marianna arranged for a complete nursery to be set up closer to your room and ordered clothes for the baby." She ticked through the list with a thoroughness that likely made governmental issues run more smoothly but felt a little steamrollerlike at the moment. She clapped her hands together. "Now if you'll pardon me, I need to pop in upstairs to speak with a judge friend of mine about something that came across my desk last week."

Ginger strode out of the office and into the hall with a fast, efficient click of her high heels.

Phoebe sagged with an exhale and turned to Marianna. "She set up all of that to happen while we were here?"

Marianna leaned closer, jostling her baby son more securely on her hip. "Money, influence and a personal assistant make things move much faster." Like with that overnight paternity test. "She means well and is usually right. You might as well go with the flow for now. If you have a stand you want to make, you'll be better equipped to do so well-rested and with a full stomach."

"You're encouraging me to leave?" She hadn't expected to find such total support within the Landis camp for whatever decision she made.

"I'm simply telling you that if you intend to fight, you would be wise to choose your timing well. The Landises are all charming—and stubborn. Of course, you're a Landis now."

"Temporarily."

Marianna didn't answer.

Realization seeped in with the full weight of what she'd done. The sense of claustrophobia she'd felt on her first night at the family compound squeezed tighter. The Landises had accepted Nina because of her blood tie. However, it was also a double-edged sword.

They didn't know Nina. So they didn't love her, not really, not yet. But they wouldn't let her go.

Kyle tossed the bouquet on the clerk's desk and picked up the pen.

The final paperwork sealing this marriage waited in front of him by the blob of yellow-and-orange flowers. Today should have taken care of all problems by securing Nina's future. His kid. His child. He still hadn't sorted through all that in his head, beyond moving ahead and taking care of his responsibilities. However, instead of smoothing out his life, this ceremony had introduced a new problem—not totally unexpected—but certainly surprising in the magnitude.

He *wanted* his wife. One kiss had made that more than clear.

His grip tightened around the pen, darkening the stroke of his scrawl. It was all he could do not to send everyone away so he could seal a deeper, fuller imprint on Phoebe's mouth and in her memory. The scent of her lingered on his shirt from the brief brush of her breasts against him and left him aching to explore. He'd found her attractive from the first time he'd seen her at the welcome-home bash. He'd even wanted to ask her out on a date.

Then they'd started talking, he'd met Nina and here they were.

At least Phoebe looked as stunned as he felt by the kiss. Thank God, he'd scrounged up enough control to keep his hands to himself so he wouldn't give the photographer an unexpected headliner. He glanced up from the paper over to Phoebe standing with Marianna. The yellow silky dress hugged the subtle curve of Phoebe's breasts, gliding over her slim hips in a way that made him wonder what she wore underneath.

Kyle checked over his shoulder fast to make sure the photographer hadn't slipped back in.

He'd been lucky to stay out of the spotlight this long, but now that he was out of the military, he was fair game for the media hounds. Although he had to admit Phoebe certainly made for a beautiful subject for the photographer with her cool, blond good looks.

Phoebe shuffled Nina over to Marianna and glided toward him, drawing his eyes to her legs. He flipped the pen between his fingers. Maybe this marriage could have some unexpected benefits. Who could fault him for sleeping with his own wife?

Her heart might well be buried along with her dead husband, but if that kiss was anything to judge by, her sensuality was alive and well.

Phoebe held out her hand. "May I have the pen, please?"

"Yeah, right." He passed it over and she leaned by him, a whiff of her floral shampoo drifting from her loose blond hair. An image flashed through his mind of the silky straight strands splayed across a pillow while he peeled her clothes away.

He tugged at his suddenly too tight tie.

Phoebe nudged aside the bouquet to rest

her wrist on the table as she signed her name. She tucked her tongue in her cheek. He could still taste the hint of coffee from her lips.

Coffee, for crying out loud. Who would have thought the simple brew would taste so sexy? His heart rate spiked.

She finished her signature with a curly flourish at odds with her no-nonsense air.

Regardless, it was official. They were married. His eyes narrowed. And he fully intended to consummate this union as soon as he could romance his new wife into his bed.

Kyle slid the papers across the table toward his mother's assistant and focused his full attention on his wife. "Have you eaten anything today?"

The family would understand if he and Phoebe opted out of any scheduled big gatherings for some time to get to know each other. He seemed to recall a quiet little café near the courthouse. He'd eaten there before with his mother's judge friend, later took the judge's daughter there for a date.

Hmm…perhaps not a good idea to take the new wife to an old date site. Moving on to plan B.

Phoebe pushed her hair behind her ears with a sigh. "It's been a busy day."

Was she thinking about her first wedding? Understandable, but he needed to divert her thoughts of the man who still had such a prominent place in her mind.

"I would offer to take you out, but I imagine you're exhausted. The rug rat looks like she needs to stretch her legs. What do you say I pick up some takeout along the way and we spend the afternoon on the beach at home? There's plenty of space away from the rest of the family so that it will be just the three of us, relaxing by the shore, getting to know each other."

"That's really thoughtful of you." Wariness lit her dark eyes. "I would like that, very much."

"Then let's get moving. Once we're past the press no doubt waiting outside, we'll be home free."

Smiling reassuringly at her, he palmed her back. This time he prepared to steel himself for the jolt of awareness sparked by the feel of her under his palm. He ushered her out of the office, into the long corridor toward the elevator. He vaguely registered the footsteps of his family following and talking with each other. Cameras started clicking again from a small pack of reporters clustered behind a security guard blocking them from pressing closer.

His oldest brother, Matthew, broke away and started speaking with one of the reporters, diverting their attention by offering up a couple of sound bites. Apparently an interview with a U.S. senator trumped snagging more photos of a surprise wedding.

Kyle smiled. Thanks, bro.

He focused his attention forward, intent on getting Phoebe and Nina home. Anticipation ramped inside him. For the first time since Phoebe Slater had blasted into his world, he had control of his life.

Nina's future would be secure.

And for however long this marriage lasted, he and Phoebe could have one hell of a totally legal affair. No worries about emotional entanglements for either of them.

He stopped in front of the private side elevator designated for employees and special guests. He jabbed the button just as the door slid open to reveal one person already inside.

Damn.

A leggy redhead in her twenties blinked in wide-eyed surprise. Then smiled with recognition.

The timing couldn't have been worse to run into one of his exes. The judge's daughter. The one he'd dated briefly in the past.

Leslie? No. *Lucy* took the bouquet from him. "Okay, Kyle Landis, you're officially forgiven." She lifted the flowers to her nose and inhaled deeply, thrusting her breasts out none too subtly. "These are just gorgeous, you charmer. Calla lilies and roses, no less. I didn't know you were so romantic."

Phoebe bristled visibly beside him, stepping away from his palm at her waist. He needed to implement damage control before some reporter with a telephoto lens and great hearing put together a new headline.

He rushed Phoebe and Nina into the elevator with Lucy and pushed the Close button. "Uh, Lucy, I'd like for you to meet—"

Lucy laughed, talking right over him. "I was just going to leave you an 'eat dirt and die, you scumbag' message, but since you've apologized so nicely with flowers," she lifted the bouquet to her nose briefly, "I'll forgive you for breaking my heart."

Five

Stuck in the elevator with Kyle, most of his family and a towering redhead holding *Phoebe's* bouquet, she mentally thumped herself for being so gullible. Bianca had warned her of Kyle's ladies'-man past, damn it.

Phoebe resisted the urge to back into a corner. Pride starched her spine. Pride, and a need to carry this off for Nina's sake.

He braced his shoulders, his uniform

stretching over his chest. "Phoebe, this is a friend of the family, Lucy Cooper. Lucy, this is my wife, Phoebe." He gestured to his daughter and said simply, "And this is Nina."

The bubbly redhead turned…well, as red as her hair. Her mouth opened and closed a couple of times, and Phoebe actually felt sorry for the woman.

Lucy's eyes dropped down to the flowers in her hand. Her mouth went tight. "I guess these must be yours. My mistake." She thrust the bouquet toward Phoebe. "Congratulations. And good luck."

There was no missing the sarcasm coating her words more thickly than her cloying cologne soaked the enclosed space in the elevator. Phoebe couldn't bring herself to be angry at the woman for spoiling the day.

She'd found out firsthand today how quickly a single kiss from Kyle Landis could persuade a woman to ignore warning signs.

The elevator doors swooshed open again blessedly soon and Lucy didn't even offer a good-bye before making tracks out into the back hall, toward a glowing exit sign.

Jonah inched forward, scratched his head. "At least she didn't ask about the kid."

Sebastian coughed into his hand. Or laughed. But Phoebe wasn't feeling the love. She couldn't avoid Kyle—they were married, after all.

However she could damn well resist his charming smile. "Kyle, I've changed my mind about dinner. I don't think I'm in much of a beach mood anymore."

Seven hours later, Phoebe dropped back onto her bed in the guest suite with an exhausted—exasperated—huff. At least she'd made it through the large family dinner, even if she hadn't been able to bring herself to eat much. Tempting thoughts of how they could have spent the evening tormented her. Images of lazing the hours away together on the beach, getting to know each other. After the Lucy debacle, he hadn't bothered bringing up cozy meals together.

She rolled onto her stomach and picked at the white piping around the dusky-rose-colored pillow sham.

Just a family friend.

How clichéd.

It was obvious *Lucy* had expected more out of Kyle, from the way she'd gushed all over the flowers. Phoebe's flowers, now discarded on the other pillow. She plucked a rosebud from the bouquet, releasing a fresh whiff of the fragrant perfume.

Stroking the bloom along her mouth, she glanced through the open side door to the connected sitting area Ginger had converted into a permanent nursery just for Nina. All that trouble and money, as if she and Nina would be staying here, made her nervous.

At least the local judge had been able to connect with a Columbia judge and they'd worked out an agreement granting temporary custody to Kyle and Phoebe Landis. Even thinking of her new last name made her shiver. She'd been Phoebe Slater since she'd married Roger. She'd kept his name even after he'd died. Before that, she'd been Phoebe Campbell. Phoebe Campbell wouldn't have been able to make things move so quickly, either, and right now she couldn't bring herself to resent the Landises for their privileged ways when it kept Nina secure.

The rest of the day had been a blur after leaving the courthouse. Ginger had had a meal ready back at the house, and neither Kyle nor Phoebe had asked to be alone.

It shouldn't matter that Kyle was a flirt with a vast dating history. She didn't intend to *stay* married to him. She only cared because of Nina, damn it, and didn't want a constant parade of countless women marching in and out of Kyle's life. Phoebe swung her feet off the edge of the bed and padded across the hardwood floor to Nina's new nursery, so much nicer than the little dressing-room nook back at Phoebe's apartment and more personal than the luxurious green nursery down the hall for visiting Landis and Renshaw grandkids.

Nina wasn't a visitor anymore.

Did she miss her tiny space back in the apartment? Phoebe had poured her heart into creating the little garden haven, complete with painted puckish fairies that reminded her of Shakespeare's *A Midsummer Night's Dream.*

This space was tastefully decorated in pinks and browns to coordinate with the already rose-colored walls. Little ballet-shoe accents rounded out the decor. Without a doubt, the Landises had more to offer Nina financially. But what about love?

Her fingers tensed along the cherrywood crib railing. Losing her husband had taught Phoebe too well how priceless and precious—and fragile—love could be. All this money wouldn't mean anything to Nina if she wasn't wrapped in affection, as well.

Ginger Landis Renshaw might be a loving grandmother, but she'd given no indication she intended to be anything other than a grandparent. And Kyle? Phoebe had definite questions and concerns about his ability to take care of Nina, if he even wanted to beyond some sense of appearances. She took her responsibility to Nina seriously.

The room darkened and she glanced up to find Kyle standing in the opening as if conjured from her thoughts. He'd changed from his suit into well-fitting jeans and a white button-down shirt with a South Carolina palmetto tree stitched on the pocket. His rolled-up sleeves exposed tanned forearms sprinkled with dark hair. Masculine arms. Even out of uniform, he made her mouth dry right up with want.

She tore her gaze away from him and gestured around the transformed sitting area. "This is lovely. The little ballet shoes are precious. Your mother and Marianna went to a lot of trouble to create this space just for Nina, when there's already a nursery here in the house."

"Marianna's an interior decorator. In fact, she decorated the whole house."

"She obviously knows her way around little-girl fashions." She trailed a finger along the tiny pink-satin slippers hanging from the wall over a mirror. "Did you need something?"

"I noticed you didn't eat much at supper. I've brought you food."

She thought of earlier, when they'd planned a picnic on the beach and considered a polite *no thanks*, but she was hungry. She simply needed to keep her guard in place. "Thank you. That's very thoughtful."

"I promised you a meal and I keep my promises." He nodded his head for her to follow him. "Let's step out onto the porch off of your room. The food is set up there so you can hear Nina if she needs you, but we won't wake her by talking."

He turned without waiting for her to answer, a man used to people following his orders, damn his broad shoulders and perfect butt. Need crackled to life inside her again with a reminder of just how much he'd moved her with one quick kiss. And she had gone so long without more than just kisses.

Stay strong. She needed to keep things simple between the two of them. Complications could spell big trouble down the line when it came time to say their farewells.

He swung the double French doors wide, out onto the veranda. "Prepare to feast."

Phoebe blinked in surprise, stopping short of the wrought iron table set with linen, silver, roses and the warm glow of a candle protected from the ocean wind by a hurricane globe. A wooden rail surrounded the balcony, the waves rolling hypnotically only a staircase away. Her dress from the wedding swirled around her legs in sensual swipes.

"This is so much more than I expected." She peeked under a polished cover and found a steak and lobster dinner, the scent of warm melted butter steaming lightly upward. "Much more."

The table was set so beautifully she'd expected some dainty, tiny offerings, and while the food was still decoratively presented, she was surprised at the hearty portions.

Kyle held out her chair. "I thought you might be hungry."

She edged past him to take her seat, her shoulder brushing him briefly before she settled into the chair. His forearms skimmed her side as he tucked her under the table, the crisp tanginess of his cologne drifting on the breeze and more enticing than any finely cooked fare.

She had to fight off the sudden urge to tip her head back against his shoulder, to revisit the taste of his mouth on hers…

"I am hungry." Ravenously so, suddenly.

Well, if she couldn't feed her senses the way her body craved, at least she could enjoy this meal. She draped a linen napkin across her lap, eyeing the cup of creamy crab soup.

Kyle motioned toward two wine bottles in silver ice buckets. "Would you prefer chardonnay or merlot?" He smiled. "Don't worry, I'm not planning to get you soused and press for my marital 'rights.' The cook just wasn't sure which kind of wine we would prefer with a surf-and-turf meal."

Marital rights.

The words brought to mind an image of the two of them tangled in Kyle's sheets, taking the attraction to a heated conclusion. Blinking back the thought, she spooned up a taste of the creamy soup instead—and held back her moan of appreciation. Then again, maybe she'd just needed an excuse to release the tension inside her at the thought of a physical relationship with the man seated across from her.

Her senses sang to life begging for more of this, of everything. "I really should keep my head clear to listen for Nina."

And to be sure *she* didn't get soused and claim *her* marital rights.

"One glass then?"

She couldn't resist *everything*. "Chardonnay, then, please."

He filled her wineglass halfway, then poured the merlot into his. He held her eyes with his while she tasted. *Damn.* There was a difference in the good stuff. How much of this would it take to ruin her for cheap wine for the rest of her life?

He set his glass back on the table. "I'm sorry about the mix-up with Lucy at the courthouse."

Phoebe tucked her tongue against her cheek while she considered what to say. She was upset, but probably not for the reason he thought. And she couldn't change anything. Better to take the high road. "You have nothing to apologize for. It's not like you were seeing some other woman while we were engaged for all of twenty-four hours."

She tried a smile, hoping the conversation would veer away from the woman.

"You're being very reasonable." He watched her through narrowed eyes.

"Did you expect me to throw a jealous fit? I seem to recall you already warned me against falling in love with you." She leaned forward on her elbows. "I'm a very good listener."

He threw his head back and laughed, that sexy sound of pure *Kyle* winding around her with the wind. "Just so you know, the wedding ring on your finger put an end to my friendship with Lucy."

"I noticed how fast she ran out of the elevator."

"I meant that as long as you're wearing my ring, I won't be seeing anyone else."

Now, that surprised her… If she could even believe him. "Bianca warned me you were a charmer."

His face hardened for the first time since she'd met him. "You think I'm BS-ing you? I may have a lot of flaws, but I do not lie."

"You really expect me to believe you're going to be celibate for the entire marriage? For a whole year?" She wondered how long he really expected that to last? Did he have plans to walk away that she didn't know about?

"Aren't *you?* What makes you think I have less self-control than you do?"

She opened her mouth—and closed it again. She didn't have an answer to that. And truth be told, as much as she cautioned herself against being gullible, she believed him on this one. Phoebe nudged aside her soup and stabbed the steak.

He swirled his merlot in his glass, watching her. "Celibacy doesn't make for much of a wedding night."

"I don't know about that." Although just the mention filled her mind with what the night could have held. Had he chosen his words with that intent? "Nina is safe for now. That means the world to me."

He finished off his merlot. "What about when Bianca shows up again?"

The bite of steak palled in her mouth. She swallowed thickly. "I only want the best thing for Nina. That would be to have her parents' love and want to take care of her."

"Even if that means giving her up?"

Her fork clattered against her plate. "Are you threatening to take her away?"

His one-sided smile returned with a dry twist. "Hardly. You're a terrific mother. But me? Ask anyone and they'll tell you I'm a crappy candidate for fatherhood."

Curiosity nipped.

"You say you're always honest, so tell me. What do you have against children?"

"Why would you say that?" he asked evasively. "Marianna and Sebastian have never voiced any complaints about me with kids."

"You pick Nina up, you carry her, even play with her, but you're always holding something of yourself back. I know it's early yet, but it seems like you distance yourself from her."

Kyle attacked the rest of his steak. "That's just your imagination."

She reached across the table and touched his wrist, stilling his hand. "I've heard too much about acting from Bianca over the years not to have picked up something. You're good, but you can't fool me."

He stared at her fingers for two crashes of the waves before setting aside his fork. "Little

Edward isn't my brother's first child. They had a baby girl before Edward, but lost her before her first birthday."

She gasped. "How awful." Her heart ached for the lovely woman who'd been so kind to her. "I can't imagine how devastated I would be if something happened to Nina."

"Sophie didn't die." But his face still creased with pain. "They'd tried for years to get pregnant, then decided to adopt. Four months after Sophie was placed with them, the birth mother changed her mind. They went through hell."

She'd assumed the extra portraits of children that didn't look like Landises were the grandchildren of Ginger's second husband. Now she realized one of the little-girl images must have been that adopted daughter. So that's why Marianna had noticed she loved Nina as much as any biological mother could. "I'm so sorry for what they went through."

"The birth mother sends them periodic updates and Sophie looks happy."

As she studied his pained expression, she realized it wasn't totally about hurting for his brother. He'd loved the little girl, too, and grieved when she was taken away. She stayed silent so he could just talk.

"My brother and his wife may be happy now, but after all they went through…" He shook his head slowly. "They even divorced at one point. My brother is a steady sort, good marriage material. Me? Not so much, even on a good day."

His line of logic wasn't going where she'd expected. She struggled to follow. "You're afraid of letting your family down?"

"I would do what I have to, but I saw from my sister-in-law, from my mother, too, how much more is needed to make a marriage and family work. I'm not cut out for that."

She almost blurted out her disbelief at his assumption, told him that he was copping out, but held the words back at the last second. He said he didn't lie to people, and maybe strictly that was true. But she suspected he was lying to himself. Men weren't always great at admitting their fears, especially if one fear involved turning his heart over to a child. "You're really content to live your life alone?"

"I have a big family around me, and a satisfying career. I have a good life."

"You seem to be forgetting one thing."

"I'm sure you'll tell me." At least his smile returned. He held her gaze over the candle-

light, the flame flickering inside the hurricane globe and casting flecks in his beautiful blue eyes.

She touched his wrist again, lingering,
feeling his pulse throb against her thumb.
"You can't escape the fact that you're already
a father."

His eyes locked on hers. Intense. In-
scrutable. Her fingers stroked along his wrist
when she'd meant to let him go.

"And you're a wife."

He stood slightly, leaned across the small
table and she knew what was coming but
couldn't find words to stop him from—

Kissing her.

His mouth fit over hers, more familiar this
time, but the tingle showering along her
nerves was still surprising in its intensity.
She'd hoped her reaction at the courthouse

had been an anomaly, some kind of mixed-up reaction to memories from her first marriage, but damn, she fit her mouth against his and wanted. *More.*

She parted her lips and he growled his approval until she could taste the rich bouquet of his merlot. His hands stayed on the table, her fingers around his wrist. He only touched her with his mouth, his tongue. The spicy soap scent of him stirred around her in the breeze, reminding her of the moment when she'd first met him and his voice stroked her senses as, temptingly, his mouth moved on hers.

She should pull away, prove she was strong and resolute the way she'd planned this afternoon. Phoebe lifted her hands to push against his shoulders.

But he pulled away first.

Her head swam and she couldn't even blame it on the drink, because he had honored her request to stick with one glass. Her only consolation came from watching his chest rise and fall as rapidly as her own. She needed to get her head together. She refused to let him win her over easily as he must have done with women in the past, like Bianca and Lucy.

Phoebe drained half her water goblet while he reclaimed his seat. She had to think. Focus on what was important.

She had to keep her head clear and her wits about her at all times. She hoped this dinner would be over soon so she could start figuring out how to deal with her desire. "Um, when do you report back to your base?"

"I've already finished up all the paperwork." He watched her, his chest still pumping. "It'll be official next week."

"So you're on vacation." And when would that vacation end? She wasn't even sure where his base was. She was married to a stranger, a totally hot stranger who turned her inside out with his kisses. The mere thought rattled her, leaving her feeling disloyal to her ex. "Rest is a good idea after such a long deployment."

"I'm not on vacation." He straightened in his chair, his eyes narrowing. "I've turned in my papers now that I've fulfilled my commitment to the air force. We were going to announce it after the party. But then you showed up with Nina, and we've been distracted since then."

A roar started in her ears, her pulse louder than the waves rushing in with inevitability. "What exactly does this mean?"

"As of today, I'm no longer in the military. I'm taking over a branch of the Landis Foundation." He spread his hands wide. "As of now, I'm totally at your disposal."

An hour later, Phoebe stood in Nina's new nursery, toying with the decorative silk slippers tacked to the wall. Control slipped away as fast as the tears down her cheeks.

What had she gotten herself into?

Swiping the back of her wrist under her eyes, she looked into Nina's crib at the sweet baby she loved so much. Phoebe adjusted the light blanket, smoothed back a dark curl…saw Kyle's one-sided smile as the infant grinned in her sleep.

Life was marching relentlessly on without her first husband. Her emotions had spiraled so far out of control she didn't know how she would ever retrieve them. Now Kyle and all the myriad temptations he presented would be with her twenty-four/seven as she settled into a family life she'd never had and that Kyle clearly didn't want.

She touched along her kissed-tender lips and searched back over their few conversations prior. What had she misunderstood to make her believe he was still in the air force, due to zip off into the wild blue yonder sometime soon? Maybe she'd just heard and believed what she'd wanted to where Kyle was concerned, desperate for a way to secure Nina's future. She hadn't looked beyond that to understand all the ways she could be hurting both their hearts to put them through this sham of a marriage.

Now it was too late to go back. She could only steel herself, forge ahead.

And try not to think about how much she wanted him to kiss her again.

Six

A week later, Kyle stood outside the nursery door, double-checking the monitor to make sure the thing was actually working. He pulled it away from his ear, looked at the buttons, clicked a couple back and forth. Yeah, he could hear the white-noise music playing low in the background.

Good God, the baby gear was more complicated than some of the intelligence equipment he'd worked with in the air force. In another week he would start with Landis International. For now, he was already unofficially working from home, but soon the traveling would start.

He hadn't lied about being at Phoebe's disposal. He just hadn't mentioned there was a deadline to that since his new job would take him on the road even more than his old one. That didn't leave him much time to win Phoebe over, into his bed.

Kyle started down the hall, eager to move forward with his next plan for persuading her they should enjoy all the benefits a wedding license brought. For the past week, he'd wined and dined Phoebe at the most romantic places he could think of, a challenge to do when considering the kid-friendly aspect. The opera had been a no go, but then he didn't really like opera. He'd even persuaded Phoebe to fly upstate on the family jet for an outdoor history fair at Halloween. He'd thought Phoebe would enjoy the historical aspect, and Nina sure looked damn cute in her little princess costume. He had to admit the kid was easier to take along than he'd expected.

Of course, he didn't really know what to expect from a child her age. He should probably get one of those parenting books or surf the Internet for kid-care articles because, his choice or not, he was a father now, which meant doing his best. He was also a husband, something he intended to focus his full attention on for the rest of the evening on their first adults-only date.

This time he would be careful not to lose control of the conversation the way he had during their wedding-day dinner on the porch. He believed they could enjoy a fun and sexy relationship. Anything more would only complicate things for both of them, not to mention Nina.

He jogged down the stairs and around the corner to the home office where Phoebe was camped out in front of the computer. A couple days ago they'd made a day trip up to Columbia for her things, including her computer for work teaching her online classes. She'd unpacked her academic gear into the honey-brown wood shelves flanking a scenic window with brocade drapes. Phoebe had added her computer to the over-large partner's desk and parked a baby swing in the corner.

He took a minute to study her, enjoying the way her straight blond hair shimmered with every move of her head, however slight. She looked every bit as enticing in jeans and a form-fitting green cotton shirt as she had in the little black number she'd worn the night they met.

While she stared at the screen, Phoebe plucked at the hair band she'd slid around her wrist—as he'd learned was her habit. He'd also learned how much he enjoyed discovering new things to entice her out of her somber reserve.

Her earthy practicality appealed to him, chasing away any initial doubt anyone might have had about her being after Landis money. She liked to walk on the beach without her shoes and bring Nina to the public park. While nannies pushed designer-clad tots in fancy strollers, Phoebe let Nina roll around on a blanket in the grass to, as she said, see the world up close.

He even liked the way her history professor side would come out at odd moments with a sudden tutorial on a historic building they drove past or a surprise lesson on the French Huguenot influence in Charleston. Jonah had snickered the first time she'd launched into one of her diatribes, but by the end, even he'd been wound up in her stories.

He couldn't remember wanting anyone this much before. "Hey, professor. How's paper-grading going?"

She glanced up, her smile quicker lately. "I've just about finished the backlog of work."

He set the nursery monitor on the corner of the desk, anticipation ramping. "Ready to take a break?"

"I'm at a stopping point. What do you need?"

He *needed* to persuade her they belonged in bed together. "Let's go for a drive along the shore."

Her face lit with enthusiasm, then she looked at the monitor. "Nina might need me."

"It's only a drive, nothing elaborate or far away. Just some grown-up time away from work. I've already spoken to Jonah and he's on his way over from the carriage house." Ginger and her husband were in D.C. for business. "He can call us or the housekeeper if he has any questions. Nina's asleep and seems out for the count." He held up the monitor, bobbling it back and forth in front of her. "I looked and listened."

"I didn't hear you." She eyed her receiver—the set had come with an extra—for the nursery monitor as if it had betrayed her.

"I was very quiet. I didn't want to wake her up." He rotated her chair toward him. "You deserve a break. Come on."

She tucked her tongue in the corner of her

cheek as she always did when mulling some-thing over, an increasingly sexy habit that left him aching to get her alone out of the house.

Phoebe gripped the arm rests with a resolute smack. "Okay, you've convinced me. Let me just save my work." She clicked along the keyboard then rolled the chair away from the desk, rising to her feet.

Stopping mere inches away from him.

Her vanilla-sweet scent tempted him to skim his knuckles down her cheek. Just one stroke. Except he didn't want to pull his hand away. She stared up at him, her pupils widening, pushing at the brown until the colors blended.

A clearing throat sounded from across the room.

Damn.

Phoebe blushed.

Kyle dropped his hand to squeeze her shoulder and turned to find Jonah lounging in the open doorway. Long hair brushed his shoulders, their rebel brother marching to his own tune, as always. "I'm ready to report for diaper duty, bro."

Kyle passed over the nursery monitor. "Thanks. I owe you."

Phoebe snagged a pencil. "I'll have all her instructions written down in just a min—"

Jonah whipped a piece of paper from his back pocket. "Already taken care of. Kyle left me a very detailed list." He glanced at his older brother. "You know I'm not ten anymore, right? Now go, both of you."

"On our way out." Kyle wrapped an arm around Phoebe's shoulders and shuttled her out of the office into the hall.

"You actually know Nina's routine." She glanced up at him, surprisingly not pulling away.

Progress.

"Isn't that why you brought her here?" He steered her down the long corridor, enjoying the familiar feel of her against his side. "To give Nina a father?"

Her smile faded and she tensed under his arm. "Has your private detective uncovered anything new about Bianca?"

"A few facts, none of them particularly helpful or I would have told you right away." He wished he had all the military intelligence equipment at his disposal now, but he could only keep tossing more money at private detectives.

What a mess for the kid. If Bianca had just gone off to party, then she didn't care about her child. And if she were dead... Either way, Nina needed them.

He was realizing more and more every day that he wouldn't let Bianca keep his child from him ever again. Even if she returned, he would still play a major role in Nina's life. "Bianca got fired a week into the rehearsals. Then it seems she just disappeared. No credit card use, nothing. But there's no indication she's met with foul play, either."

"That's a relief at least." Phoebe grasped the banister on the way down the winding inside stairway that led to the garage.

"At least the judge is on our side with the temporary custody order."

She glanced over her shoulder at him. "How long do you think we'll need to keep up this charade?"

"Let's just take it a day at a time." He swept

open the garage door. "Or rather, one evening at a time." He palmed her waist on his way past the SUV for towing the boat and on down the line of family vehicles.

Phoebe tapped his hand on her shoulder. "Kyle? Kyle, that's your Mercedes."

"We're not taking it." He passed his car and stopped in front of their ride for the night. "I leased this for a few days."

A 1965 Aston Martin convertible.

"Oh my God," she gasped. "James Bond style."

He opened the passenger door and passed her a scarf. "Let's make it a ride to remember."

After settling in behind the wheel and maneuvering out of the estate, he opened up the engine on the shoreline road. She threw her head back with an abandon that stirred thoughts of uninhibited sex. He downshifted around a curve, houses spacing farther and farther apart until there was nothing but shoreline stretching ahead.

She hooked her arm along the open window, her hair and the scarf streaking behind her. "This is amazing."

"Wait until I drive you along the shores of Greece."

She laughed, along for the fun of the daydream. "Then we could go to the Parthenon. I've always wanted to see it for real."

"I can make that happen tomorrow."

Phoebe pulled her arm back inside. "Nina has a well-baby checkup."

"Then we'll go the next day." He slowed the vintage car, angling off to the side of the road, easing to a stop. He needed to recapture the joy on her face from earlier. "What else is on your tourism wish list?"

Her face creased with incredulity. "Well now, if we're dreaming, let's dream big." Her eyes tracked fast as if she was overwhelmed by the possibilities. "I'd want to see all the regular stuff, Big Ben, the Eiffel Tower, but mostly I want to see the street-side cafés, the people, the feels and tastes of the…" She shook her head, scooting down in her seat. "I'm being silly."

"Not silly at all. Seeing the world has always helped me put life into perspective." His job as head of the international offices for the Landis Foundation offered a lot of travel, the main reason he had been all right with ending his military career.

Phoebe wrapped her arms around her waist as she took in the open marshlands on one side of the car and boats bobbing on open water on the other. The humid air hung heavy through the evening and brought cooler weather. "Thank you again for the outing. I can't believe you planned this for me. It's perfect." She turned her head along the back of the seat to look at him. "You've really been wonderful all week. I appreciate your trying so hard."

"Don't go getting soft on me now. Remember that love talk we had."

She thumped his shoulder, laughing. "Egomaniac."

He laughed along with her, wondering how in the span of just a week it could have become so important to him to see her smile. Her eyes held his. She stilled, waves crashing in the silence between them. He angled to kiss her and found she was already on her way over to meet him halfway.

A kiss. Just a kiss but the feel of her soft lips against him stirred him more than… Hell, he didn't want to think about anyone else. Only her and how damn good she felt against him. Her breasts brushed his chest, and he had to feel her skin. Now. He skimmed his hands under the hem of her cotton shirt and stroked up her back, urging her closer to him. Not near enough.

The sexy sound she made—a high sigh, half moan—sent his hand higher to span her back and feel every available inch of her. His heart rate kicked into overdrive faster than the Aston Martin, all systems go. He'd waited for her ever since that kiss on their wedding day, but it felt as if he'd been waiting forever.

If he could guide her across to straddle his lap—

She nipped along his mouth and rested her cheek against his, her breath gusting over his ear. "We can't do this."

His pulse was more jacked than if he'd run all the way here, but he slowed his breathing to try and rein himself in. He'd hardly done more than kiss her, yet she had a way of shredding his restraint. He caressed up and down her back, massaging. "I have birth control in my wallet."

Phoebe buried her face against his shoulder. "That's not what I meant. It's too soon. We've only known each other a week."

Hadn't he thought the same thing a few seconds ago? But he couldn't bring himself to fuel her argument. "We're married adults."

Arching back, she cupped his face, her hands firm. "Do you have a hearing problem? I've only known you a week."

The real answer knocked around inside his head. "You're not over your dead husband."

She flopped back in her seat and shouted to the open sky, "Damn it, Kyle, I've only known you a week!"

"How long had you known him?" Frustration—and, hell yeah, jealousy—made him push when he damn well knew better.

Phoebe hesitated so long he wondered for a minute if she was simply going to blow off his question. He was just about to start the car again when she sighed.

"I'd known him all my life," Phoebe said softly. "He told me he loved me the first time when we were seven years old and I fell off my bike. We had a great marriage right up to when he died five years ago." She looked down. "That probably sounds corny to a cynic like you."

It sounded exactly like the sort of unconditional commitment a woman like her deserved. "My parents had that kind of marriage before he died. She loved him so much I didn't think she stood a chance at finding it again. But man, was I wrong." Her stillness stopped him. "What?"

The moonlight illuminated the confusion in her eyes. "You're making an argument for falling in love twice, but I'm not supposed to fall in love with you."

Ah, crap. "Wait, uh…"

"Gotcha." She winked.

And that surprised the socks off him. "You're wicked, Phoebe Landis."

"Not really."

Something had shifted between them when she'd opened up enough to talk about her past and, all jealousy aside, he wasn't letting that progress slip away. He draped an arm over the steering wheel. "Oh, I think you've got a seriously untapped bad girl in there."

She tightened her wispy scarf around her head again. "Well, I can tell you for sure you won't be tapping any of that tonight."

He let his gaze wander over her, begrudgingly enjoying this bold, confident side of her. At least her eyes didn't have that haunted look anymore. In fact, with her swollen lips and tousled hair, she appeared vibrant. Vital. And very, very touchable.

Good thing he already had his hands on the wheel.

Kyle cranked the engine. He would let her go for now, but he had hopes for a lot more next time. "Lady, you're killing me here."

"Somehow, I believe you'll survive until morning."

"I'll be thinking of you all night." And he'd

already arranged it so when she climbed in bed, she would find a surprise gift that ensured she would think of him, too.

Seven

"Thanks, Jonah," Phoebe said softly, walking up the side steps to the porch just off her suite. The sandy wind stung her legs, her skin still overly sensitive from one sensory-igniting kiss. When he didn't answer, she moved closer, reassured by the steady drone of the nursery monitor on the table.

Her brother-in-law sprawled in a chair at the table, his head back and eyes closed. His laptop computer also rested on the table, open to a full-screen shot of a girl with a backpack, a panoramic mountain range in the background.

Curiosity drew Phoebe closer…Jonah's eyes snapped open. She stepped back, embarrassed to be caught staring at him when he was apparently resting his eyes. "Pretty girl."

"Nice ride?" he asked, dodging her comment and clicking the photo closed.

What was his life like when he wasn't surrounded by his ambitious and well-connected family? "Lovely ride. The shoreline view is gorgeous. Thank you again for keeping an ear out for Nina. Did she give you any trouble while we were away?"

He glanced past her as if to check for Kyle. She was alone, though. Kyle was putting away the Aston, since she'd bolted from the vehicle as quickly as she could rather than risk being tempted further.

Jonah passed her the nursery monitor. "The munchkin didn't make a sound the whole time. But don't worry, I still looked in on her twice."

She tapped the top of his computer. "Checking your MySpace?"

He tucked the laptop under his arm. "Grad school paper. Thank goodness for laptops." Jonah winked on his way past and down the steps, looking so much like Kyle—except for the longer hair. "G'night, Phoebe."

He loped across the manicured lawn toward the carriage house, keeping his secrets. She wondered if Kyle knew more about the girl on Jonah's screen saver. They seemed such a close family. How easy it would be to grow too comfortable here and forget it was all temporary.

Phoebe wrapped her arms around her waist,

wishing it were that easy to hold together the pieces of her tattered control. She'd played things light with Kyle after his kiss. She'd sensed that would be the best way to gain some much needed distance.

His surprise ride along the shore in the vintage auto had touched her far more than any five-star dinners. Without question, the quirky car pick appealed to the history buff in her. He'd chosen his venue well for softening her up.

Time to return to reality. She eyed the nursery monitor, then raised it to her ear. Lullaby music played in the background, but she needed to see her girl to be sure. She creaked open the nursery door, leaned inside and, sure enough, Nina slept soundly as Jonah had said. The little one sucked her bottom lip, snoozing away.

Phoebe closed the door softly, suddenly awake and restless. Maybe she should try to get more work accomplished, except she couldn't scrounge up enthusiasm for chaining herself to a desk, especially after the open-air outing.

Might as well just curl up in bed and try to sleep, since Nina would be awake early. Phoebe pivoted toward her bed…and stopped short.

A large gift, wrapped in rose-patterned paper, rested on top of the pink-and-white accent pillows. Cocking her head to the side, she approached the package warily. Who?

She plucked the card from under the bow and found it simply read: *Enjoy! Kyle.*

Her skin began tingling again in excitement as she picked up the briefcase-size box, testing the weight. Heavier than she would have expected. She didn't dare shake it without knowing if it was fragile. She peeled back a piece of tape slowly, careful not to tear the paper. It had been a long while since someone had surprised her with a present.

Phoebe parted the floral wrapping, taking her time in the unveiling...of...

A laptop computer.

Her nerves tingled hotter, tighter, his thoughtfulness touching her as firmly as any stroke of his hands. How had he pulled this off? She glanced at the porch. He must have left the gift with Jonah to place on her bed.

Kyle had put even more planning into the evening than she'd first realized. He must have noticed her struggling to balance work with caring for Nina. The new computer would make her life so much easier. Possibilities bloomed in her mind. She could even write on the patio, with Nina in her swing.

Phoebe smoothed her hands along the box, the night stretching long and lonely ahead of her. She knew full well what she was missing in turning him away.

Her cell phone rang from inside her purse. She looked at the clock—11:42 p.m.—and smiled. It could only be Kyle this late at night.

She fished the phone from her bag and, yes, his number scrolled across the faceplate. Dropping onto the edge of her bed, she answered. "Thank you so much for the computer. I should say it's too extravagant, but it'll help me spend more time with Nina so I can't bring myself to say no."

"I was counting on that. And you're welcome." His bourbon-smooth voice intoxicated even through the airwaves.

She sagged back on the pile of pillows. "Why are you doing all of this? I would have taken care of Nina without all the kindness." Silence vibrated through the phone and over her nerves. "Kyle?"

"I'm here. And I think you know exactly why."

Her mouth dried up with the possibilities, dangerous possibilities that could threaten her objectivity. "Sex would complicate things between us. We wouldn't be able to go back. That could make things very awkward living together."

"Would it help you to know that my new job is with Landis International? I'll be traveling a lot, starting next week."

He would be leaving soon? She inched up higher on the pillow stack, not sure how she felt about this latest revelation. "All this romance has been about a short-term affair?"

"You've made it clear you aren't interested

in any emotional commitment." He paused while his words sunk into her brain, tickling her mind with the possibilities. "Five years is a long time to go without sex."

There was only one way to deal with Kyle. Surprise him, keep him as off balance as he kept her. If that was even possible. "Who says I've lived like a nun since my husband died?"

"Are you sure about that?"

"Of course I'm sure." She'd dated and even tried to take things to that level, only to bail before making it to the bedroom. "I've learned to take care of those needs on my own."

Had she really just said that out loud? At least she'd managed to shock him silent. She gripped the phone until her fingers turned blue.

"Damn, Phoebe," he growled low. "You're trying to kill me, aren't you? Because an image of you 'taking care of yourself' could definitely give me heart failure."

She burrowed deeper into her pillows, her face heating with embarrassment—and stirring excitement. "I can't believe we're even having this discussion."

"Then I'll let you go…for tonight. See you in the morning."

She thumbed the off button and clutched the phone between her breasts, right beside her pounding heart. Her way of dealing with Kyle proved to be a double-edged sword. In spite of her best intentions and how little time they'd known each other, she wasn't sure how much longer she could hold out against the allure of Kyle and a short-term affair.

Four days later, Kyle buckled the seat belt in the Landis family jet, preparing for takeoff.

Finally, he had Phoebe to himself after an evening of family attendance at a diplomatic dinner in D.C. at the infamous Watergate Hotel. Phoebe had agreed to come along when she'd realized they could fly there and back in the same evening. Nina would only be with a sitter for a few hours, mostly asleep. Time management had been better for Phoebe overall with the computer, so she'd agreed.

His pulse kicked up a notch just remembering their phone conversation the night he'd given her the new laptop. Finding ways to romance his wife had been an exciting challenge, but he was beginning to get a sense of the things that appealed to the history major in her. He'd initially planned on skipping the D.C. function because of the distance from home, and the temporary custody order mandated that Nina stay in state for now.

Then he'd thought of the family's private jet.

The event had been important for Landis contacts and he'd been surprised how much he enjoyed having her by his side. His brothers and their wives had stayed in D.C. to visit longer with their mother and her husband. Sebastian and Marianna had a sitter who traveled with them. Maybe next time Nina could go with them and they could spend the day in the Smithsonian—

Next time?

He should be focusing on the present and the stunning woman in the seat next to him. Her hair sleekly upswept, Phoebe stared out the window at the night sky as they left the nation's capital behind after an evening of dancing.

The vibrantly red satin gown hugged her elegant curves, the strapless cut revealing a hint of the gentle swell of her breasts. Landis diamonds around her neck and dangling from her ears refracted the muted overhead light as if the stars from outside had come inside. The European ambassadors hadn't been able to keep their eyes off her.

The intercom system crackled to life. "Mr. and Mrs. Landis," the pilot's voice filled the cabin, "we're at cruising altitude. You are free to walk around."

Kyle unbuckled his seat belt and strode toward the galley kitchen. "There's a midnight snack here if you're hungry."

He'd planned ahead for this private time with Phoebe. The pilot was in front behind a closed partition, and a sleeping compartment was built into the back behind another partition. He really didn't need to think about the bed a few feet away. Not yet, anyway.

Phoebe unbuckled her seat belt and stood,

stretching with a sensual moan of pleasure that shot straight to his groin.

"Thanks, for the food, for the whole evening. This is so surreal," she twirled in the middle of the floor, her hand sweeping toward the sofas lining one wall and the rows of leather seats on the other, "having a baby-sitter while we jet up to D.C. for dinner and dancing, home before Nina even wakes up."

"I'm glad you enjoyed yourself. You look…" He took in the curve of her exposed neck, her creamy skin glowing against the deep red strapless dress. "Absolutely amazing."

"And thank you again. You look very handsome yourself, Mr. Landis." She stepped closer to him, toe to toe, and tugged his tuxedo tie straight again. "Do you miss your uniform?"

He stilled under her touch, careful not to startle her away. "Do you?"

Some women were downright groupies when it came to military men. The person inside didn't matter to them, only the trappings that came with the job.

She patted his chest once before backing away. "You're just as good-looking in the tux as you are with the medals, and you know it."

His chest still bore the phantom feel of her touch, his skin warm under the stiff fabric. But he was making progress, so he let Phoebe have her space. He pulled the protective wrapping off a silver tray of brie, bread and fruit, and opened a chilled bottle of sparkling water. "You must really think I'm egotistical."

"I think you're confident and sexy and exasperating." She plucked a purple grape from the platter and popped it into her mouth. "So you're okay with hanging up your uniform?"

He barely registered her words, so caught

up in watching the way her pink lips moved, enticing him to kiss the sheen of juice from her lips. Then he saw she was waiting for his answer.

"Sure, I feel nostalgic about turning a page on that chapter of my life, but honestly, I never planned on the air force being a career."

"Then why did you join up if you always intended to get out before retirement?" She leaned a slim hip against the marble counter dividing the kitchen from the seating area.

His gaze lingered on that hip as he imagined his hand molding to fit the curve of her waist and trail lower to explore.

He filled two cut-crystal glasses with ice, then water. He wanted something stronger, but he needed a clear head around this woman. "It was about serving my country, about giving something back."

"That's really admirable." She studied him with curious eyes before looking away self-consciously. She reached for her water glass. "I read up on you before I came here, and I saw that you were in a plane that was shot down. There wasn't a lot of information in the article. The writer noted something about withholding details to protect you while you finished your tour of duty. I wondered if the crash had anything to do with your decision to get out of the service."

That day smoked to life in his memory like a dark but distant cloud. "Definitely not the highlight of my life, but I know I was lucky. Not a scratch on me. Apparently someone lurking around on a mountain shot down the plane. Everyone survived the crash landing, but we had to abandon the site to hide out from rebels. So the rescue mission took a while longer."

Her hand flew to her neck, her face creasing with concern. "Those hours must have been horrifyingly long for you. How did you get through it?"

He spread brie over a cracker slowly, his mind awash in memories. "We all opened up an MRE—meal ready to eat—and thought about our families back at home. As I sat there, crunching on the rat-nasty crackers, I kept remembering how Sebastian and I used to eat peanut butter and marshmallow sandwiches when we were kids."

"That must have been frightening wondering if you would see them again."

It had been total hell. He offered her the cracker and cheese, surprised to see his hand was steady.

He lost himself in that past memory to distract himself now, as he had in the desert.

"This one time when I was about ten and he was nine, we spent most of the summer playing in a forest behind our house. Well, it seemed like a forest, anyway. It was probably just a few trees with a bike path."

"Haven't you always lived at the Landis compound?"

"My grandparents used to live at the compound. We moved in when Dad got out of the air force and ran for senator. Dad said we needed the extra security the place afforded, but I sure missed the freedom of our old digs."

"That sounds like a haven for children." She brushed a cracker crumb away from the corner of her mouth absently, her eyes locked on him.

Kyle picked up his water glass, swirling the lime around and around. "We would hang out in 'our woods' all day long. We'd pack marshmallow and peanut butter sandwiches, take a gallon jug of Kool-Aid. And we dug tunnels."

"Tunnels?" she nudged gently.

"We dug deep trenches, put plywood over the top, then piled dirt to finish it off." He could almost smell the musty little cavern. "We were lucky we didn't die crawling around in there. We could have suffocated, or the roofing could have given way if someone had accidentally stepped on one of those boards."

Shivering, she wrapped her arms around herself, plumping her breasts in an understated but alluring display. "What did your mother say when she found out?"

His eyes flicked over her neckline and he closed his hands against the impulse to learn the shape of her firsthand. He knocked back half a glass of water. "My mother never knew about the tunnels. She would have grounded us until we left for college if she had." And they would have deserved it. His mother had been tough but fair. "We made Jonah stand guard and let us know if she was coming."

"How much did you have to pay him not to snitch?"

"Who said we paid him?" He winked. "He's the youngest. He did what we said."

She leaned closer for another grape, her vanilla perfume drifting over him. "And your oldest brother, Matthew?"

"He's too much of a rule-follower. We never let him in on the secret. I was especially into it—I would sneak out there on my own sometimes. Sebastian says it's no surprise I went into the military."

"So you're all four even closer now that you're adults." Her gaze danced down to her glass of water. "I envy that kind of love and support."

"We're lucky. I was lucky that day in the desert. I thought about those sandwiches a lot while I waited in that trench in Afghanistan." What would he think about if the same thing happened today?

Without question, he knew his mind would be packed with images of Phoebe and Nina. They'd both filled his world so damn quickly, an unsettling notion given how short a time they'd both been in his life.

Phoebe rested her hand on his by the silver platter. "It's really honorable that you served your country. You had any number of options and you still chose to give back."

He flipped his hand to link fingers, her soft skin, her warmth, and just that fast he found himself imagining how much softer her skin would be under the dress. "Or maybe I just didn't know what to do with myself after graduation."

She shook her head. "If that had been the case you could have simply lived off your trust fund."

"Boring." He shrugged off her compliment, uncomfortable. He stroked his thumb over her wrist, enjoying the way her pulse leapt under his touch.

Her pupils widened with awareness, but she didn't pull away. "What about your new job? Will it keep you from being bored?"

This whole conversation was getting deeper than he'd intended. He didn't want anyone picking around inside his brain, getting closer, especially when he knew his lifestyle and hers ultimately wouldn't be compatible for anything more than a casual affair. They needed to keep emotions well clear, for Nina's long-term benefit. He also needed to get this conversation, this whole outing, back on track.

Still holding her hand, he tugged her nearer until her breasts brushed against his chest. His body tightened instantly in response. "You know what would keep me from being bored right now?"

Her head tipped back, exposing her neck as she stared up at him with intense dark eyes. "Stop it. I want to talk. If you really want to stand a chance at getting me in bed, then be serious for just five minutes."

Phoebe's words stoked his barely banked desire. "You're entertaining the possibility of us in bed?"

Eight

Standing in the jet cabin with her emotions as firmly in the clouds as her body, Phoebe couldn't deny it any longer. She wanted to make love to Kyle. And yes, there was a part of her that was comforted by the fact that he would be leaving soon. The aftermath would be simpler with time to regroup. Maybe, just maybe she could keep her heart safe this go-around.

The whole outing had been surreal from the start. She'd never imagined flying in a private jet, wearing such extravagant jewels or hobnobbing with international dignitaries in a historic hotel ballroom. But the man more than the accessories had made the evening. Kyle had been at his charming best, his smile and strength reminding her at every turn of the pleasure waiting a simple stroke away.

If she dared.

She knew without question if she didn't take this chance now, she would regret it for the rest of her life. Kyle was right. She was on fire with unfulfilled needs, needs growing increasingly painful the more time she spent with him.

Committed, nervous—excited—she flattened her hands to his chest again. "As soon as we land, I want us to be together, to consummate this marriage."

His eyes went sexy lidded as he slid his hands around her back, angling her hip-to-hip against him. "Who says we have to wait until we land?"

The possibility of having him now, here, sent a surge of thick longing through her veins. But her ever-present practicality tapped her with reservations. "What about the pilot?"

"He's behind the partition and has his hands full flying the plane. Even if he needs to switch to autopilot and open the door for some reason, he would announce himself over the intercom first," Kyle explained. His hands roved up the zipper along her spine and down her bare shoulders, callused fingertips rasping over her skin with tantalizing masculinity. "The bedroom in back isn't large, but we'll have privacy, atmosphere and protection."

Need gathering speed inside her, she eyed the small door behind the seats. She hadn't paid much attention to it on the flight down since his brothers and sisters-in-law had been along. She also hadn't realized then that she and Kyle would be flying back alone.

Very alone. No more waiting and second-guessing.

Delicious anticipation sent her arching up on her toes until his mouth waited a whisper away from hers. "Then, yes, I'm more than *entertaining* the idea of us going to bed together."

His hands spanned her waist and he lifted her up onto the counter island. He stepped between her legs, his breath warm and seductive against her brow. "Stay right there, just where you are, so I can touch you," he sketched his lips over her brow, "feel you," he kissed over her cheek-bone, "take my time with you."

He sealed his mouth to hers, his tongue searching, soothing and exciting all at once. The thready reins on her restraint snapped. She'd been thinking of him, of this, ever since that night he'd given her the laptop, the night he'd told her she would be in his dreams. She looped her arms around his neck, desperate to get even closer still. The silk tuxedo lapels under her soothed along the overheated flesh of her exposed shoulders, the fabric a sexy, extravagant luxury for such steely strength.

His fingers traced just below the diamond necklace, dipping between her breasts far too briefly. Dragging in breaths between frenzied kisses, she inhaled the scent of his aftershave, gloried in the scratch of his rougher cheek against her skin.

Hot sensation spiderwebbed over her skin, a network of exquisite pleasure from the barest of touches. He cupped her face, brushing kisses over her eyes and cheeks while he stroked her exposed shoulders until her breasts ached for his attention. She linked her ankles behind his knees and urged him nearer, as close as he could come with her gown bunching between them.

Growling his appreciation, he inched the hem of her dress up to her knees, freeing her to wrap her legs around his waist. He cupped her bottom and lifted her off the counter.

She squealed into his mouth, then held on tight as he walked across the cabin toward the door. He opened the door to the sleeping compartment, angled inside and kicked it closed again with a final click. The double bed invited with its thick burgundy comforter that brought out the warm glow of mahogany accents and brass-globe lighting. Dim light, but just enough for her to make out the hard lines of desire etched in Kyle's features as she sprinkled kisses over his face.

He lowered her to her feet, sliding her body down his with sensual precision. "Patience, Phoebe."

"Later." She swept aside his tuxedo jacket, burning to see him, *have* him.

He tugged the zipper on her dress down her spine until the air gusting from above chilled her back. She trembled in delicious anticipation. *Finally.* His warm, bold hands tunneled inside, lower, lower still until he cupped her bottom and brought her against him for another moist, searching kiss.

Rational thoughts scattered as quickly as their clothes hit the floor—both his clothes and hers—and before she knew it, cool air blasted over her bare breasts. She tightened in response, her senses humming as surely as the engines powering them through the night sky.

His eyes roved her body as she stood clad in nothing more than her champagne silk panties and a fortune in diamonds. "What was that I said about patience? I can't seem to remember right now."

Reveling in the mutual attraction, she kicked aside her dress pooled at her feet and savored staring at a gloriously naked *man.* If she'd had more space, she would have stepped back and simply admired him. Instead, she traced the angular line of his jaw, down to the hard plane of his collar-bone, over his pectorals. His muscles jumped under her fingertips.

He stepped closer, his skin sealing against hers, the hot, hard length of his desire pressed to her stomach. Kyle walked, backing her until the edge of the mattress hit behind her knees. She toppled onto the bed and he followed her down, ducking his head in the tightly confined space.

The small cavern with curved walls, engine droning, gave her the sense of being closed off from everyone and everything. They were truly in their own private haven.

He stretched over her, leaning on his elbows to hold the bulk of his weight off her. She hooked a leg around him, pulling him full out on her. She wanted all of him, the full-bodied experience of him blanketing her.

He palmed just below her breasts, stroking his thumbs along the sides, then around to her already tight nipples. The pressure of his gentle torment made her ache for more and she arched against the warm pressure of his leg between hers. His blue eyes darkened to near violet, broadcasting just how much he wanted her, too.

Her eyelids went heavy, and she couldn't stop them from closing even as she mourned losing the vision of him over her. Other senses heightening, she inhaled the tangy scent of him mixed with the musk of desire. Part of her felt the frantic edge of passion clawing to get free, but she gritted back the impulse to rush. Reality would take over soon enough.

She felt the hot gust of his breath an instant before he took her mouth. He kissed her, long and well with the talent of a man who knew how to please.

Tasting the pungent, buttery flavor of brie, she explored just as deeply. He stroked her breasts with persistence until she wriggled against him, hungry for deeper pressure. And she could tell without question he wasn't unaffected. The hard swell of him throbbed and she ached to learn the intimate feel of him.

Phoebe slid her hand between them and encircled his hard length, slowly caressing until he rolled onto his side, taking her with him. She considered tumbling farther so she could be on top. A quick glance told her the angled ceiling was low enough that if she lost control and arched back she could bump her head. A definite mood buster.

She draped her leg over his, understanding now why he'd shifted, and she found she liked the equality of power in the position so very much, especially when he hooked his thumb along the low waistband of her underwear. Her hand stilled, every nerve ending focused on where his search would lead him next....

Yes.

Two thick fingers dipped inside her panties,

his touch cool and welcome against her over-heated flesh. He stroked, parted, found the tight bundle of nerves. Her hands fell away and she gripped the comforter, tighter and tighter until her muscles burned.

Faster, but softer he circled until frustration knotted within her. She nipped his lip. He growled lowly, trailing his mouth away, along her neck. She gasped, again, and couldn't stop the moan that followed. If she didn't find relief soon, she might well scream.

"No more teasing. Finish this. Patience is for later, remember?"

"Whatever you say, whatever you *want.*" He traced the curve of her ear, his promise stroking her senses as surely as his hands, his tongue, even the enticing brush of his body against her.

Still, he wouldn't allow her the release she

craved. She let go of his hip and tried to slide her hand between them again to torment him as fully as he was tormenting her. He clasped her wrist, halting her progress.

A whimper slid past her lips. "No more."

"Do you want to stop?"

"No! I mean, no more playing." She stroked the full length of him.

He groaned. "We're in agreement on that."

If nothing else.

But she didn't want doubts or darker thoughts now. She needed—deserved—this stolen moment of pleasure with him. He thumbed either side of her panties and skimmed them down. His hands came back up and somehow he'd palmed a condom. Before she could chase that thought further to a time when she'd considered getting pregnant, Kyle sheathed himself and pulled her to him again.

Side by side, he nudged against the core of her, entering, stretching, her body oh-so-sensitive from such a long stint of abstinence. Gasping, she went boneless from the sheer pleasure of the thick pressure. She slid an arm over him, her fingers threading through his close-shorn hair.

He whispered in her ear, words of encouragement, of how much he wanted her, how she turned him inside out. Each sexy sound stroked her emotions as smoothly as he stroked her body while they rocked against each other.

She'd wanted him since hearing that sexy voice of his for the first time. It had been so damn long since she'd even felt desire, much less pursued it. The rippling, sweet surge of sensations stormed through her as she writhed against him. She pressed her face against his neck, grasping him with frenetic hands, her nails scoring down his back.

Too soon, the storm gathered in that tightening swell and as much as she wanted to delay, she lost control. She clasped him closer, harder. Her teeth clamped into his shoulder with the force of her completion exploding through her. He thrust harder, faster, drawing out her orgasm until every nerve tingled, damn near burned until he followed her over the edge.

Slowly, she realized her arms were locked around him, the vent chilling the light sheen of sweat slicking her body and his. He rolled to his back, hugging her to his side. His chest still pumped heavily and she couldn't have found the air to talk even if she knew what to say. She wasn't even sure what to think.

She was too busy being scared. Because without question, she'd found so much more than she'd expected to experience here with him. Ever with anyone. At an earlier, freer time in her life, she might have taken a chance on this man with potent kisses, restless feet and a carefree smile. A risky proposition, to say the least.

With Nina's stability at stake, Phoebe feared she couldn't risk another night in his bed.

After their jet landed and they gathered their luggage, Kyle opened the car door for Phoebe, enjoying the way the moonlight played with her loose hair. Hair loose and fluffed from lovemaking.

Before they'd even had time to steady their breathing, the pilot had called over the loud-speaker, announcing they were preparing to land. Phoebe had launched from bed and shimmied into her dress again.

He'd known she had a passionate nature beneath her cool exterior, but he hadn't had a freaking clue how much steam waited to be tapped. His body surged with the memory of how she'd fit against him, of how she'd responded. Of how damn hot she'd looked wearing nothing but diamonds and a light sheen of perspiration. His back bore the marks of her pleasure.

And he looked forward to adding more as soon as they both recharged with a few hours' sleep.

He slid into the driver's side of the Mercedes. "We'll be home soon. I've already arranged for someone to come by in the morning to watch Nina so you can sleep in."

She looked at him sharply. "Thank you, but I'd rather not. I've already spent enough time away from her."

He drove out of the small airport's parking area and onto the main highway. "I can see how that would be upsetting for Nina."

"It's more than just not wanting her upset. She's had enough shuffling in her life as it is." Phoebe shoved her hair back from her face, frustration sparking in her eyes as clearly as the diamonds refracting the dash lights. "Don't look at me like I'm being overprotective."

Had he done that? "Sorry." He reached across to tunnel a hand under her hair and massage the back of her neck. "I only wanted to make sure you had enough rest."

She tucked her tongue in the side of her mouth. "I'm the one who should apologize for snapping. You were just being thoughtful." She sank back into the seat, easing away from his hand. "I'm so afraid of doing something wrong with her. Before Nina came into my life, I knew so little about babies. As Bianca started depending on me more and more for babysitting, I did research to make sure I had all the most current information."

Good God, if she inched any farther away from him she would fall through the open car window. What the hell was up? Suddenly her speed in getting dressed and out of the jet seemed like evasion rather than efficiency.

He needed to keep her talking and hopefully clear the furrows from her brow before they got home. Before they went to bed. "How did you and Bianca end up friends— and staying friends? You're both so different."

"We met in a theater history class in college. Roger was a theater major, too, and I took the class to be with him." Streetlights whipped past on the nearly deserted road.

"We met Bianca and we all hit it off. She's more the flamboyant type and I crewed backstage for a couple of productions, building sets, making costumes."

"What about Roger?" He stomped back any residual jealousy and watched her out of the corner of his eye.

"He was a playwright, a really gifted one." She thumbed her wedding ring around and around. "I've always thought he would have made it big if he'd lived."

He couldn't miss how she talked about both Bianca and Roger being the spotlight sort yet didn't seem to see her own special individuality.

"We all three had such big plans and dreams in those days." She looked down and he wondered if she felt some of the same jealousy he'd wrestled with. "I'm not really sure why I've kept in touch with her, but I'm glad I made the effort for the occasional lunch out to catch up. Otherwise, I never would have known Nina." She looked over at him, full on for the first time since they'd made love. "What are you thinking?"

"That maybe you kept up the friendship with Bianca in spite of your differences because you weren't ready to let go of your husband." Downshifting around a corner onto a two-lane road, he hated the image coming together in his mind. "Being around her made you feel connected to him. This way, you don't have to let go and move on."

Pain flashed through her eyes. "Wow, that's pretty insightful for a card-carrying member of the testosterone club."

"That's me—Mr. Sensitive." What would have happened if he'd met Phoebe instead of

Bianca? "So you've researched Mommying 101."

"There's a lot of information out there, scary information."

He pulled up outside the security gates leading into the Landis compound. "You still look worried."

"Of course I'm concerned about her future," she said as the iron barriers swung open. "We may have kept her safe today, but until we know where Bianca stands, there's still so much uncertainty. I guess what worries me most is the uncertainty. If Nina is meant to be with Bianca, of course it will break my heart to let her go, but it's more important that she be settled somewhere, securely, permanently."

"Even if it's with Bianca?" He guided the car along the winding drive, oak trees and palmettos lining the way.

"Even if. There are so many frightening studies out there right now about attachment disorder. Have you heard of it?"

"Only in very general terms. It has something to do with kids not bonding, right?" He pulled up outside the garage.

"A lot of the studies focus on babies that are neglected or abused. When they don't learn to bond as babies, it affects how they can bond as children and adults." She turned to face him, her face shadowy in the dark garage as the door closed behind them. "Nina hasn't been neglected or abused, but some of the studies also suggest there could be attachment issues when babies are shuffled from caregiver to caregiver, never having a chance to bond with anyone."

"And that's what you worry about with Nina."

She stared down at her hands, twisting the

diamond-studded wedding band around her finger again. "All babies deserve security. I would do anything to keep her safe. *Anything.*"

Just that fast, it hit him. Even if he'd met Phoebe before, she might not have even consented to a date. She'd only married him because of Nina. Her loyalty to Nina—to her dead husband even—might not extend as far as him.

Anger crackled inside him over the idea of just how far she may have been willing to go to secure Nina's future. "And was tonight about doing anything to make sure you don't lose Nina?"

Her eyes went wide and her mouth fell open. "Are you insinuating I would sleep with you just to keep Nina?"

Kyle scrubbed a hand over his unshaven face, reason poking through his anger. "Of course not. I know you better than that." His hand fell away and he cupped the back of her neck again. "I'm trying to figure out why you're pulling away after some of the most amazing sex ever."

She looked away, but at least she didn't dodge his hand this time. "This is difficult for me, being with someone again." A long swallow moved her throat. "You've always had a large family to depend on, so maybe you don't get what it's like losing the only person in your world. We only had each other. He was a foster child and both my parents died before I finished college. Dad died from complications during a routine surgery and Mother basically grieved herself to death."

"I'm sorry." He started massaging her neck again, finding deep and unrelenting kinks.

"It was a long time ago, but I still miss

them. Especially at times like this. They would have enjoyed Nina so much." She smiled bittersweetly. "But you understand that, don't you, having lost your father?"

He nodded, his dad's death still as tough today as it had been when he was a confused and grieving teen. How much worse it must be to lose a spouse. "How did your husband die? You said he drowned, but there must be more to the story than that."

She blinked fast even though her eyes were dry. "We'd both been working too hard. I was finishing up grad school, and he took on a second job to help pay my tuition. We decided to spend an afternoon at the beach. The day was beautiful, sun shining, but the wind was heavy, making for red-flag swimming conditions. So we just picnicked."

"What went wrong?"

Fresh tension kinked in her neck under his fingers all over again. He resisted the notion there might be nothing he could do to help her through this.

"Two tourists tried to surf the waves in spite of the warning. One of the guys got caught in the riptide and called for help."

"Your husband answered the call." God, he couldn't even resent the guy anymore.

"He would have made it out, too, but the surfboard hit him on the head. It was a freak accident."

Still, she blinked fast against dry eyes and he realized she'd already cried herself dry over the man.

"You really loved him."

She nodded simply, reaching up to link her fingers with his. "Love that strong doesn't just go away." She cleared her throat and plastered a brittle smile on her face. "So don't worry about me misunderstanding what happened back in the airplane. I understand our marriage is short-term. You've made that clear enough from the beginning."

"What if we stayed married?" The words fell out before he'd even formed the thought. But once said, it made total sense. "We've got a great thing going here. Amazing sex, a friendship, security. We're both so independent we won't need to live in each other's back pocket. You want clear? Okay, let's stay married."

She watched him with sad eyes. "What about love? You might find it one day and be sorry."

"No," he insisted, backing away from even the thought. "I have my future mapped out and it's too transitory for any woman to put up with. We'll have different expectations in a partnership."

He didn't know why this mattered so much, had never thought about extending the marriage before now. But the possessiveness fisting in his chest wouldn't retreat.

Kyle angled closer, the perfect argument coming to mind to win this battle. Defeat was suddenly, deeply unpalatable. "You could have more children one day. You're a natural mother."

She gasped. In shock or horror? "Are you presenting yourself as a sperm donor?"

"What if I'm offering that, and more?" His question filled the space between them with possibilities.

And she didn't say no outright. Confusion scrolled across her face and he prepped his next line of persuasion. Victory hovered so damn close—

The phone rang from the depths of her bag.

She startled in her seat. "That can only be about Nina this late." She avoided his eyes and dug in the bag at her feet until she found her phone. "Hello?"

"Phoebe?" a female voice shrieked so loudly from the other end of the line Kyle could hear clearly. "Phoebe, is that you?"

The voice slammed him back in his seat. It couldn't be. Not now. But Phoebe's terrified eyes confirmed what he already suspected.

Bianca was alive and well on the other end of that phone line.

Nine

Frozen in the front seat of the Mercedes, Phoebe gripped the phone, terror and relief warring within her. Kyle tensed beside her and she feared he might reach for the receiver.

Her fingers trembling, Phoebe changed to speakerphone. "Bianca? Is that you?"

"Of course it's me," her college friend, Nina's mother, answered. Her perfectly modulated voice filled the car. Any accent had long ago been smoothed away in her theater training. "I'm standing outside your apartment. I've been ringing your doorbell for the past five minutes and the neighbors are starting to get pissed. Wake up and let me in."

Bianca was in Columbia? Where had she been all this time? Wherever she'd been hiding out, she must not have read a newspaper if she didn't know about Phoebe and Kyle getting married. The news had been splashed all over South Carolina and beyond. Diplomats from around the country had congratulated them last night at the D.C. dinner party.

A marriage they'd consummated, the scent and feel of him still lingering under her satin gown. Had it only been a few short hours ago they'd left for Washington, D.C.? Good God, her world was blowing apart faster than she could gather up the pieces.

At least Bianca seemed oblivious to all the changes that had gone on in their lives, which would give them a few precious hours to get their thoughts together before Nina's mother burst through the door. "I'm not at home. I'm in Hilton Head—with Nina."

She couldn't even think about the upheaval this would cause for Nina. She'd just been settling into the Landis home and their new—more secure—life. Phoebe's belly clenched.

"Hilton Head?" Bianca asked. "What are you doing there?"

Phoebe glanced at Kyle beside her in the parked car inside the lighted garage. How would Bianca react to the news they'd married? Even more important, didn't Bianca care what had happened to her child? Of course not, or she wouldn't have simply disappeared. "I'm taking care of *Nina.*"

"Oh, how's the kiddo doing?"

The throwaway tone grated along Phoebe's already raw nerves. It was obvious Bianca was unharmed and had chosen to fall off the face of the earth.

Phoebe resisted the urge to throw the phone as maternal anger mushroomed inside her. "Nina's fine. Since you left her with me last summer, she learned to roll over. She's almost sitting up on her own."

"Good, good. Thanks for babysitting. Do you have an extra key hidden around here somewhere? It's not under the flowerpot like it used to be, and I really need a place to crash."

Babysitting? Babysitting! Two months—nearly three months now—went way beyond some kind of nanny gig, especially with an infant.

"I took the key with me when I left my apartment." She'd closed up the place but had kept paying rent. She'd planned on going back, but deep down she'd always thought Nina would be with her. Now Nina had both her biological parents in the picture, which left little room for a *babysitter.* "Uh, Bianca, I'm in Hilton Head with Kyle Landis. When you didn't come back, I brought her here to her father."

She watched Kyle's jaw flex, his face stark and hard, anger darn near rolling off him in waves. Nina would have a fierce defender in her Landis father. Silently Phoebe sent up a prayer of thanks that she could count on him now.

"He's back from Afghanistan?" Bianca's voice breezed from the phone. "Wow, cool, I was planning to get in touch with him."

How could she be so blasé about letting Kyle know about his daughter? Would Nina have ever had the chance to know this big and wonderful family if Bianca hadn't told Phoebe?

He gestured for her to keep talking.

Phoebe swallowed down the wad of fear clogging her throat. "Well, you can come to Hilton Head and talk to him in person."

"He's probably mad, isn't he?" Bianca asked, hesitancy tingeing her voice for the first time. "Could you just bring Nina back here?"

Phoebe's patience snapped. If Bianca thought she could steamroll over her old, quiet friend, she was in for a rude awakening. "I can't do that, Bianca. You abandoned your daughter. Kyle has temporary custody."

"Phoebe," Bianca gasped, "what in the hell have you done?"

"You didn't leave me any choice when you walked out on your child."

"Fine, I'm getting a hotel for tonight. I'll meet you in Hilton Head tomorrow."

It was less than three hours' drive. Nothing would have stopped Phoebe if it were her child, and oh, God, she could lose Nina now. "Call when you get close to town and I'll give you directions to the house."

Bianca hung up without another word.

Phoebe stared at the phone in her hand, a chill settling all the way to her bones. Her teeth started chattering. Vaguely, she heard Kyle speaking to her, offering up soothing words about how everything would be okay. But she couldn't think of anything but checking on Nina.

Phoebe tossed aside her phone and bolted from the car. Bunching her dress up, she raced into the house, up the stairs, not stopping until she reached Nina's nursery.

The crib was empty.

* * *

Kyle heard Phoebe's scream.

He sprinted into the nursery and found her clutching a baby quilt to her chest as she stood by the crib. "Where's Nina?" Panic lit her eyes as she looked frantically around the nursery. "You said she would be taken care of. I shouldn't have left her for even a second. Oh, God, do you think Bianca lied and she's already taken her?"

Kyle cupped her shoulders. "Calm down, it's okay. Nina is in the main nursery. The sitter put her there and went to sleep on the daybed. Nina hasn't been alone for even a second since we left."

Phoebe sagged with relief. He pulled her to his chest, understanding her fear and vowing for her—for Nina—he wouldn't let anyone harm one hair on their heads. She shuddered against him, and it ripped him up inside to see his normally cool wife fall apart.

With a final trembling sigh, she straightened. He only had a second to register her damp eyes before she charged out and into the hall. Her high heels clicked along the hardwood floors as Kyle followed her to the green nursery his mother kept for all her grandchildren.

Phoebe cracked the door open slowly— warily?—and peered inside. She slumped against the door frame, her eyes closing, releasing two fat tears. "Thank God."

Kyle stopped behind her and peered through the door at the baby fast asleep in the spindled crib.

His daughter.

He allowed himself a selfish moment to just stare at Nina and reassure himself she was okay, she would be okay. He memorized her features, a face he should have studied more fully before now.

She had the Landis chin and hair. If she were awake, he would be staring at his own eyes. But beyond that, he knew she liked her feet uncovered and she giggled when he waved her favorite panda-bear teething toy in front of her face.

It was so damn little to know. He should know more. He *would* know more. He wouldn't be that part-time parent jetting off for months only to find out his child had met a milestone while he was gone. He had options, damn it.

She was his daughter.

He loved her. And in the morning, he could lose her to a woman who didn't think anything of disappearing for nearly three months. He'd never known this kind of fear before, not even when he'd been shot down in Afghanistan. The full impact of that crushed his chest until he damn near couldn't breathe. He couldn't even imagine what kind of hell Phoebe must be feeling. His wife had loved this little girl for months.

He started to reach for Phoebe, but she stepped deeper into the room. She quietly called out to the sitter, gently waking her, smiling her thanks and telling her she was free to go to the guest room across the hall.

Once the sitter bustled past him and into the other room, Phoebe curled up in the corner of the daybed as she'd done her first night here.

Watching her distance herself from him, Kyle realized he wasn't just in danger of losing his daughter, he could also lose his wife.

* * *

"I'm here to pick up my daughter."

Bianca strode into the foyer of the Landis mansion, flicking her wavy red hair over her shoulder with a gesture Phoebe recognized as calculated to catch male eyes. It usually worked.

At least today, Kyle seemed oblivious to Bianca's dubious charms, currently encased in skinny jeans and a lime-green tank top. His barely banked anger steamed behind his eyes. Nina didn't seem to notice the tension, however, as she patted him on the face with her panda-bear teether clutched in her chubby fist.

Even as tense as things were between her and Kyle, Phoebe was relieved to have his support in this standoff with Bianca. He'd called the rest of his family this morning and they would all return within hours.

Kyle palmed Phoebe's back. "Let's all step into the living room and talk. There's a lot to go over from the past few months."

Bianca eyed the wide-open entryway, her deeply tanned fingers gliding over a blue-and-white Fabergé egg by a crystal vase of lilacs. She strolled deeper into the living room. A wall of windows let sunshine stream through and bathe the room in light all the way up to the cathedral ceilings. Hardwood floors were scattered with light Persian rugs around two Queen Anne sofas upholstered in a pale blue fabric with white piping. Wingback chairs in a creamy yellow angled off the side. The whole decor was undoubtedly formal, but in an airy, comfortable way.

Phoebe feared Bianca was seeing dollar signs. But if she'd only wanted money, wouldn't she have come to Kyle right away?

Bianca spun on her spiky green high heel and extended her arms. "My baby." She gripped Nina so firmly Phoebe had no choice but to let go. "Aren't you beautiful, and so big?"

"Yeah," Kyle muttered, "they grow. As a matter of fact, they grow a lot if you don't see them for nearly three months."

Phoebe rested a hand on his arm, wary of angering Bianca, especially when they didn't have a clue what she had in mind. "Where have you been? Do you realize how worried we've been?"

"Were you worried about me, or did you just care because of Nina?" Lifting an eyebrow, she hitched the baby on her hip awkwardly. Nina squirmed and threw her panda-bear plastic teether on the floor. "It doesn't matter now. I'm back and ready to see my girl."

Kyle stood, feet braced, in the archway between the living room and foyer as if blocking any chance of escape. "You fell off the face of the earth so completely we thought you might be dead. You still haven't told us where you were."

"Sorry about that. I went to the islands with this important director. He said he had a part for me." Bianca pried Nina's fingers off her giant gold-hoop earrings. "He lied, the scum, but I got a vacation out of it. Mothers need vacations. I'm all rested now and ready to snuggle with my little girl."

Phoebe resisted the urge to grab Nina and run. "You can't just abandon Nina for months and think I'll trust you to take care of her."

Bianca looked back and forth between Kyle and Phoebe standing close together. "Ah, I see how it is." She jostled Nina uncomfortably as the baby tried to climb down. "You've got Kyle now and if you lose the kid, you lose him. He's quite a catch. I can see how you wouldn't want to give all that up."

Phoebe bit back the impulse to snap at Bianca. Kyle was more than some "catch." He was about so much more than his bank balance. He was an honorable man who cared about his family, took his responsibilities seriously and even appreciated the simple beauty of beachside rides in an open-air car.

Kyle scooped up Nina's plastic teething toy from the floor and lifted Nina from Bianca's awkward hold. "Phoebe and I are married."

Bianca blinked fast, speechless for once.

His daughter secured against his chest, Kyle waved the tiny panda bear in front of Nina's face, soothing her into precious baby giggles.

"She came to tell me about Nina, and we found we had a connection."

"You expect me to believe you two fell in love? You're kidding, right? Phoebe's totally locked in the past with Roger." Her painted lips curved with a hint of condescension as she turned to Phoebe. "And let's be honest, girlfriend, you're not exactly Kyle's type."

Phoebe rocked back a step at the blatant cruelty of her so-called friend's words. She'd maintained the friendship with Bianca because she was outgoing and vivacious, a force that had pulled Phoebe out into the world when she'd felt isolated by grief. And yes, maybe she'd had blinders on where Bianca was concerned because she'd been part of happier times in Phoebe's life. But the blinders were off now.

Bianca winked. "Maybe you can get something in the divorce settlement. You married him to help his daughter, after all. What?" She blinked with overplayed innocence. "That's why you married him, isn't it? It's not like the two of you knew each other."

A brief flash of anger iced Kyle's eyes before he smoothed his features into a neutral mask. Phoebe admired his calm, his skill in putting feelings in the background to remain focused on solving the problem. She could see well what had made him such an effective warrior.

Kyle's gaze pinpointed on Bianca. "What do you really want?"

"My baby."

Cold fear sprinkled goose bumps over Phoebe's arms. "The courts have given Kyle temporary custody. You left her. We'll need to go back to court to settle that."

"That's really upsetting." Her look went calculating. "You actually care about her already? She is a pretty kid."

Her worst nightmare was unfolding. Again, she was losing someone she loved, and while she tried to console herself that at least Nina was alive, Phoebe still couldn't erase an image of the baby crying out for her at night and wondering... The pain went deeper than tears.

Bianca, however, blinked big, fat tears down her face. "I'm so sorry. I've been so stupid, but I really thought I could make a better life for Nina. I'm not good enough for her, not like you and your family."

Was Bianca acting or had Phoebe grown more cynical?

If only she didn't know what a damn fine actress Bianca could be. Had she been using those acting skills on Phoebe all this time, too?

Had the entire friendship been a lie? Perhaps Kyle was right that she'd clung to Bianca out of a need to hang on to the past with Roger. She'd allowed herself to be blinded.

Phoebe gathered her shaky poise. "Where are your bags? I'll show you to your room."

Bianca shook her finger. "No, no, no. I'm not staying here under your judgmental eyes, with you recording every misstep I make. I'm staying in a hotel and Kyle's paying." She passed Kyle a card. "Here's the number so you can call with the specifics."

She hitched her bag higher on her shoulder and twitched toward the door. The closing door echoed in the silence.

Swaying, Phoebe could have sworn all her bravado melted from her. She grabbed the wingback chair behind her and sat heavily.

Kyle paced around the living room with

Nina, still waving her panda toy in front of her face. "Phoebe, I don't want you to worry. We'll play this out in the legal system. The judge isn't going to reverse the custody arrangement on a whim, and I doubt Bianca has the staying power to hold out long-term."

Phoebe wasn't so sure. The cynic inside shouted Bianca was ready to dig her spiked heels in deep. But she let Kyle continue to spell out his plans, realizing that taking charge seemed to keep him calm.

She watched him stride back and forth across the room, Nina cradled confidently against his chest. When had he grown so comfortable with her? There was no mistaking the connection as Nina stared up at him with adoring blue Landis eyes. He waved her favorite panda-toy teether in front of her face, joggling the beads in the panda's clear belly around in a gumball-like display. Nina loved that toy.

And Phoebe couldn't deny the truth any longer. She'd fallen in love with Kyle.

Ten

He'd never felt so out of control.

An hour after completing their meeting with the judge, Kyle clenched the steering wheel, driving the Mercedes along the dark shoreline with Phoebe beside him. The car seat in the back was empty.

The judge had awarded Bianca one-night-a-week temporary visitation with Nina, starting today. The judge had given them the next month to gather information or work out an agreement before he revisited the case.

Thank God for Sebastian's artful negotiations or things might have played out so much worse. He'd managed to wedge in a provision. Kyle would pay Bianca's expenses and hire a nanny to stay with Bianca and Nina during the twenty-four-hour visitations. At least they had the reassurance the baby would be cared for, and Bianca couldn't skip town with Nina. They'd all stayed at the courthouse until arrangements had been made with the sitter they'd used during their D.C. trip.

He'd done everything possible for now. And still, it didn't quiet the roaring inside him. The sun sank as hard and fast as his gut. What if they still lost Nina? The love he felt for his daughter slammed through him all the more once he had to watch

Bianca walk away with his little girl. Seeing the devastated expression on Phoebe's pale face at the loss had only hammered home his failure.

His headlights swept around the next curve, sharper than he'd expected, and he forced himself to slow down. He wouldn't be any good to Nina or Phoebe if he totaled the car. His hands shook so hard he decided to pull off the deserted road until he regained control of the fears broadsiding him.

Kyle guided the sedan onto a secluded parking area sandwiched between dunes with towering sea oats. The wind tore in off the ocean, bits of spray pinging on the windshield.

His hands fisted against his knees, tighter, tighter again as if he could somehow hold back the swelling frustration inside him. Muscles tensed and bunched up his arm until he slammed his fist against the dashboard with a curse.

He welcomed the bolt of pain that shot up his arm. He considered giving the leather a second go…until he saw the tears streaking down Phoebe's face.

Ah, hell. Those tears hurt him far more than if he'd broken his hand. "I'm sorry, Phoebe, so damn sorry."

Sorry for more things than he could even put into words right now. He gathered her against his chest, and she didn't even protest, just sagged against him. A choking sob caught in her throat. She gripped his suit coat until her fingers dug into his shoulders, the same fears and frenzy radiating from her that he felt inside himself. He thumbed away two tears streaking down her cheek, rested his head against her brow, murmuring whatever consoling words he could scavenge out of his own stark arsenal.

Phoebe burrowed closer, turning her face toward his caress, toward him. "Touch me," she whispered, her voice hoarse and agonized, "hold me, make the emptiness go away."

Kyle stilled. She couldn't possibly be suggesting they...

But then she pressed a kiss into his palm, her lips moving against him as she spoke, "I can't stand one more moment thinking about what happened. I need you to give me something else, something wonderful, to think about."

All his frustration gathered force with a purpose—giving Phoebe the distraction, the outlet, even a momentary relief from the pain. He guided her face up to his. Their mouths brushed. *Held.*

Phoebe's fists unfurled from his suit coat

and her fingers crawled across his back to clamp him closer. Passion exploded inside him, feeding off all the frustrated emotions that had stockpiled within him since Bianca's out-of-the-blue call. Hell, since Phoebe had shut him down after sex in the airplane.

Kyle slid his hands up to cup her face, to fit their lips more surely against each other, to deepen the kiss and contact and connection. All the frenzy of the day channeled into the moment, seeking an outlet.

He grazed his fingers down her back to cradle her hips, guiding her onto his lap the way he'd fantasized about doing when they'd made out by the shore in the Aston. But, where that night had been about seduction, this moment was about release.

She slid over his legs, her pink-cotton wrap-around dress bunching up around her hips.

The fabric parted along the side at the wrap, exposing her rose-colored panties. He slipped his fingers along both hips, twisting the silky fabric until the underwear…snapped. He brushed aside the scraps until she pressed against him, moist and hot.

She sprinkled desperate kisses along his mouth, his jaw, nipping and tempting with her tongue and teeth. The last rays of sun faded. The dusk of night sealing them in darkness, heightening his other senses as he inhaled her vanilla scent mixed with the musk of sexy want.

Her panting breath synced up with his. Phoebe tore at his belt, making fast work of his fly and freeing him from his boxers. She stroked him, already throbbing and hard in her hand. The touch of her cool fingers spiked his need. He clenched his teeth, scavenging for bits of his shredded control long enough to fish his wallet from his back pocket. His eyes adjusting to the dark, he plucked out a condom.

She rocked her hips against him, her body bare and welcoming. His jaw flexed, his throat moving in a slow swallow as his lashes went heavy for an instant and he fought the urge to close his eyes.

He tore open the packet. "Wait."

"No patience tonight." She snatched the birth control from his hand.

"I agree."

"Now shh…" She rolled the condom along the length of him, urgently, efficiently.

Phoebe straddled his lap, kneeling over him as she positioned herself. He cupped her buttocks and guided her down on him until they sat together, connected. Cradling her in his palms, he thrust and she writhed and they moved in tandem, knowing each other's bodies and needs better this time.

She squeezed her arms tighter around him, echoing the clasp inside as well that urged him closer and closer to completion as surely as her breathy moans and sighs and demands for *more, harder, faster. Now.*

Wind rolled in off the ocean, carrying salt and sea spray through the vents. Their mating was raw and sweaty and intensely consuming. It went beyond sex. It was different being with Phoebe, and that scared the crap out of him, because if she left, nothing would be the same, nothing would be as good.

Her moans grew louder, louder till the sound of pleasure filled the car. She clawed at his shoulders, anchoring herself deeper as he watched the shadows play across her face, watched her come apart. Her breasts thrust forward with the powerful arch of her spine again and again, her neck exposed in a graceful arch. He felt the damp strength of her release. She contracted around him, massaging him…over…the edge.

His head dropped against the seat rest. He rode the surging release rolling in wave after wave of expanding explosions. He wasn't even sure anymore if the roaring in his ears came from the ocean or his own body.

He combed his fingers through her hair, her face tucked against his neck. They hadn't solved anything out here by the ocean, but at least she wasn't crying anymore.

He dropped his chin to rest against her head.

Damn it all to hell, what a time to understand her powerful connection to her dead husband. Because right now, Kyle knew he would find a way to make her love *him,* no matter how long it took.

Phoebe had to do something, anything.

The pure helplessness of waiting to see Nina home again safe and sound was eating her alive. Sitting cross-legged on her bed, she clicked through the keys on her laptop computer, surfing the Internet for anything she could find on child-custody battles. She needed to arm herself with as much knowledge as possible. Kyle, too, had his laptop out, but he'd set up on the patio outside her suite. Only a few more hours and they would pick up Nina.

Neither of them had strayed far from Nina's room. Did he feel closer to their daughter here, too? She couldn't even hazard a guess. Since they'd made such frantic love in his car, Kyle had completely shut down. He'd spent most of the night working at his computer, even after his family had returned. He'd surprised her when he'd climbed in bed with her at about two in the morning, making slower, more thorough love to her with his body, his mouth, his words, but said nothing about his own needs or pain. But being with him hadn't distracted her from worrying about Nina as much as it had rocked her to the core.

She'd felt Kyle's hurt for his daughter, the raw edge to his lovemaking. That shared connection had dissolved her defenses against him, leaving her open and so much more vulnerable than she'd ever imagined.

Then she'd woken alone. Gazing across the room to the open balcony door, she found him on the porch back at his computer. He'd pulled away again, and she didn't know why. She could understand his frustration over losing full custody of his daughter, fears of the next judge's hearing upsetting Nina's world even more. But his retreat seemed motivated by more than that, since it had only grown deeper after they had made love.

She swung her feet to the floor and padded across to watch him through the open French doors. A light breeze fluttered the whispery curtain and lifted her hair, the air muggy after the night of rain.

What would Kyle do if she walked up behind him and massaged the tension out of those braced shoulders of his? Maybe it was worth the risk to find out. She stepped outside only to pull up short when she saw the deep furrows in his brow. "What's wrong?"

"Take a look at this." He turned his laptop screen toward her, displaying an image of Bianca at a beach party, dancing between two men, an umbrella drink held over her head. "Does that seem like Bianca was working to make a better life for her child? Check out the time stamp."

Less than a week ago.

"There are more. Lots more. And not just drinking, but drugs and even a sex tape that, uh…" He pinched the bridge of his nose, shaking his head. He clicked the drop-down menu to save the latest Internet site, his jaw flexing but his eyes still flat and emotionless. "It appears she didn't spend much time wasting away missing her child."

The crowded party and cabana sure looked like it provided phone service, yet she'd never bothered to call. Phoebe pulled out a chair and sank down beside him. "Why didn't the private investigator find these?"

"Most of them are from the past week. And

I have some, uh, skills from my military intel days." His fists clenched on the table, his wedding band glinting in the high-noon sun. "Damn it all, I should have been doing this myself from the start."

"You've been doing everything you could to take care of Nina from the first moment you met her." She slid her hand over his fist. "This is scary stuff. Thank goodness you found it now."

He slipped his hand from under hers and clicked through more computer commands. "I need to do more. Time's running out."

"When do you leave to start your new job?" It seemed he'd already left emotionally now. The fragile common ground they'd just begun to share seemed to be slipping away as surely as the cresting waves pulled sand from the shore.

"I've pushed back all my meetings until we get things settled with Bianca. I meant that time is running out for Nina."

"What if it takes a while to settle the custody issue?" A frightening possibility they both needed to face.

"It won't," he said curtly. "I won't let it."

She touched his wrist, trying again to break through the icy exterior that only cracked during sex. "Some things are beyond even the control of a mighty Landis."

"The great thing about being a Landis is that we're all equally as determined. I have a wealth of support when it comes to being there for Nina."

"When it comes to your daughter, there's no replacement for you."

He turned suddenly-haunted eyes on her. "You think I don't know that? I've already told the family I'm not taking the job heading up Landis International. I have options, and I intend to make the most of them."

She was stunned at this abrupt shift in his life plan. "But surely you can just postpone it. You won't be happy nailed down to one place, you've said so yourself. There has to be a better compromise. Let's talk this out."

"There's nothing to discuss."

She leaned closer, refusing to let him push her away. She'd fought for Nina and she would fight just as hard for him. "Kyle, damn it, you're the one who keeps preaching to me about not shutting down, about coming back to life."

Something smoked through his eyes and for a moment she thought she might have truly gotten through to him. Then his beautiful blue eyes iced over again.

He shoved his seat away, iron grating across

stone tiles. "This isn't about me. We're in the middle of a custody battle. Unless we work together, presenting a unified front in our marriage long-term, we could well lose Nina for good." He closed his laptop and stood. "We should get moving so we're not late picking up Nina."

He left her sitting on the porch alone and confused. As she sat, stunned at the loss of lighthearted Kyle with his bolstering one-sided smiles, his words trickled through, about staying a married couple long-term.

Finally he'd committed to staying together, yet she'd never felt farther apart from him.

Eleven

Sitting in an antique rocker in the living room, Phoebe cradled Nina in her arms even though the baby had gone to sleep at least fifteen minutes ago. She hadn't been able to let her out of her sight since they'd picked her up yesterday. The room was silent but for the rustling of her mother-in-law at the coffee table, pulling Thanksgiving decorations from a plastic storage bin.

Phoebe couldn't help but be warmed by the lack of pretension in such a powerful world figure. Wearing a lightweight orange sweater set—and blue jeans—Ginger Landis Renshaw could have been any other grandmother preparing for the holidays with her family. What would it have been like to have such a woman to turn to after Roger had died? Or when she'd been wrestling with what to do after Bianca had disappeared?

Kyle was sequestered with his brother. Maybe he would find some comfort and reason there since Sebastian would understand the pain after having lost his adopted daughter. Heaven knew Kyle still wasn't listening to her. His emotional retreat from her stung more than she could have ever imagined a few weeks ago. How had she opened herself to so much pain again?

Phoebe rested her cheek against Nina's head and inhaled the sweet scent of baby shampoo, watching her mother-in-law lift out a brass cornucopia. "That's a beautiful piece."

Ginger glanced over her shoulder with a smile before placing the horn of plenty on the mantel. "It belonged to my first husband's grandmother. She loved the holidays. She also gave me the most exquisite family Nativity, a magnificent collector's piece. It's in a museum now, but I had a replica made for my grandchildren to enjoy."

"How lovely to have such long-living traditions in your family." She glanced down at the wedding ring Kyle had placed on her finger, over the spot that had once worn Roger's simpler gold band. "Forgive me if this is too personal, but did your husband—

the general—ever have a problem being reminded of your first marriage?"

Ginger turned slowly and leaned back against the cool hearth. "Hank and I have been friends for years, back when we were both married to other people. I helped him with his children after his wife died. He helped me after I lost Benjamin. This love we've found came later and certainly surprised us both, pleasantly so."

"No jealousy then?"

"None. That doesn't mean we got over losing a spouse quickly. When I say it took us a long time to find each other, I mean a very long time. Years. Yet here we are, blending our Nativity scenes and families." She patted Nina's diapered bottom. "I look forward to setting up the crèche with my granddaughter someday."

"Make sure you take pictures, lots and lots

of them." In case Phoebe wasn't a part of her day-to-day life anymore. Regardless of Kyle's talk of working together, she didn't have faith in the long-term hope for their relationship.

"I have photos in the album of my boys setting up the Nativity with their grandmother. In fact…" She leaned into the container, sifting through padded ornament holders. "I believe the replica ended up in here with the Thanksgiving decorations."

Ginger straightened, holding a velvet bag in her hands. "Here we go." She sat on the edge of the sofa and began withdrawing the wrapped pieces. "Matthew and Kyle used to argue every year over where to put the Wise Men. Matthew is such a traditionalist like his father. He wanted them right there in the manger. Kyle, however, pointed out that the Wise Men really didn't show up until two years later, so they should be positioned somewhere outside the manger."

Phoebe rocked Nina, eyeing the trio of porcelain figures and envisioning a young Kyle dreaming of the Wise Men's world travels. The reproduction of the antique crèche still looked vintage, with an Old World style to the rich-hued paints.

Ginger cupped a camel in her hand. "Every year, my little smart-aleck son would cradle those three porcelain antiques and shake his head, saying, 'Two years, for Pete's sake. That makes 'em the three wise slackers, if you ask me.'"

"That certainly sounds like Kyle." At least the Kyle she'd known a week ago. Would Nina have his sense of humor, as well as his smile? Would they see that humor again?

Ginger placed the camel behind the three

kings. "He always has joked to cover when he's uncomfortable with emotions. His father being gone so much bothered him deeply, but Kyle always shrugged it off as if it didn't matter."

Could he be shutting down as a different defense mechanism against uncomfortable— hell, painful—emotions? He was all action, without a doubt, and she'd learned long ago men sometimes overcompensate with actions at the expense of words and feelings. "Kyle turned down the job with Landis International."

Ginger didn't look up, just continued to arrange the figures on the coffee table even though it was weeks too early for Christmas decorations. "I was disappointed to hear that. I take it he seems to think he can't be a good father and travel the way he wants."

"He even hinted that leaving would be the same as what Bianca did." She thought back to the time she'd expressed her fears about attachment disorder and how that must have fueled Kyle's concerns. "Have you ever talked with Kyle about this? Maybe he'll listen to you."

Laughing lightly, her mother-in-law shook her head. "If I've learned anything in all my years parenting and in politics, it's that you can't tell people anything and have them accept it as truth. They have to come to the conclusion on their own."

"But you told *me*."

"You were almost there on your own and you already had all the pieces in place."

Phoebe tried to understand where Ginger was going with her trip down memory lane, but the way she saw it, things looked so damn bleak. "Are you telling me this so I can give up on Kyle?"

Ginger leaned back on the sofa, her blue eyes wise but kind. "I'm helping you so you can show him the pieces he needs to put it together." She gave the camel a final nudge so it lined up alongside the magi. "It may take a while, even a long while, but don't give up. Some people see the pieces differently, but as long as you're both talking about how to work it out, you'll find the answers that are just right for you."

Phoebe looked at the porcelain set resting on the coffee table. She could almost see the four Landis siblings taking turns arranging the figurines, the brothers so alike in looks, but different in many ways now that she knew them better.

And what about her? How would she have displayed the scene? No matter how many times she jostled it around in her head, she couldn't recreate what she'd put together before. Her mind kept envisioning things differently, from the perspective of a mother, with Kyle's quirky, slacker Wise Men off to the side.

Slowly her vision cleared and the image of how her life should be came together again, differently than before, with Roger, but no less wonderful. She wanted a future with Kyle, a unique life together that they built, not some attempt to recreate the past. Something was going on with Kyle, but not for a moment did she believe he didn't care.

The time had come to truly take command of her life and be the wife and partner Kyle deserved.

Kyle sensed a new determination in Phoebe as they sat around the table in the courthouse mediation room to discuss the first round of custody specifics with Bianca. Kyle had buried himself in paperwork in the hopes that he could make this right.

He'd vowed he would do anything to make Phoebe happy and look toward the future rather than the past. Keeping Nina absolutely topped the list of securing everyone's happiness. After they'd crossed that hurdle, he would do everything in his power to be the best husband and father possible—even if that meant nailing his ass to a desk in Hilton Head.

He just hoped the evidence they'd found about how Bianca had spent the past months would turn the tide in their favor. So much depended on the judge's final verdict, and Sebastian had told him that could swing either way. Still Phoebe sat next to him exuding quiet confidence, her chin high and shoulders square.

Bianca huffed a ragged strand of hair off her brow, thumbing through the stack of documents in front of her. "This is all so complicated and official."

Phoebe leaned closer to Bianca. "You have to understand we only want to keep Nina safe."

"That's what I want, too," Bianca rushed to answer. "I just want to play with her."

Kyle started to reach for the file of damning photos. Phoebe placed a hand on his arm. "Wait a moment." She leaned on her elbow. "Bianca, do you truly want custody of Nina?"

The confidential tone in her voice was soft. Nonaccusatory. And completely caught him off guard. What the hell was she doing? Even ever-stoic Sebastian tensed in the leather seat.

Bianca scratched mascara from the corner of her eye, her gaze darting around nervously.

"What kind of mother doesn't want custody? Even you want her and you're not her mom."

"No one here is judging you, Bianca," Phoebe continued with admirable calm. "We all want what's best for Nina and best for all of us, including you. Why not let go of who you think you should be. Be who you are and let's work from there."

Kyle's neck started to itch. Phoebe had said much the same thing to him when he'd told her about turning down the job with Landis International.

Phoebe reached across the table to Nina's biological mother with an openness Kyle didn't think he could have scavenged.

"Bianca," she pressed gently. "What's really going on?"

Bottom lip quivering, Bianca squeezed Phoebe's hand. "You're going to think I'm an awful person. All of you." She looked around the table. "Nina's sweet and I do want to see her. But I want to be an actress. That's all I've ever wanted." She blurted, "I need money."

Sebastian's eyes narrowed.

Anger gelled inside Kyle as what he'd feared and expected played out. "You want a payoff."

Phoebe touched his leg lightly under the mahogany table, patting his knee reassuringly to quiet the storm brewing inside him.

"No, no." Bianca raised both her hands defensively, her long, manicured nails reflecting the halogen bulbs overhead. "I'm not bribing you. I wouldn't do that. I may have flaws, but I would never sell my baby. I just want a decent shot at being an actress. I've got an audition in Bollywood and I can't afford the plane ticket. All I want is a plane ticket."

Bollywood? In India?

Kyle stared at her in shock. She was already making plans to jet? To leave their daughter all over again? But on the plus side, all she wanted was a damn plane ticket. Less than a thousand dollars. If Bianca was interested in bribing them, she would have asked for a hell of a lot more than that.

Bianca twisted her hands in front of her, a blur of fuchsia nails and silver rings. "I realize you're pissed because I didn't tell you about Nina, but I knew if I came to you, you would get all wrapped up in making a family. I mean, God, all you talk about is family, family, family." She glanced up quickly. "No offense meant to any of you."

Sebastian smiled, one-sided. "None taken."

"Anyway, I didn't know what to do and Phoebe's so smart and logical, I knew she could take care of everything. I'm not like her.

I'm not cut out to be a full-time mom, no matter how much I love the little cutie."

Kyle vaguely registered his wife murmuring something about how glad she was to take care of Nina, furthering his sense that Phoebe undoubtedly had Bianca's number.

Had Bianca even somehow set this whole thing up, arranging circumstances so Phoebe would come to him? Kyle couldn't go quite that far, but he could see he had sure sized this up way wrong from the minute Bianca had walked into the Landis home.

Sebastian began speaking with Bianca in his best soft and reasonable lawyer tones, explaining the ins and outs of what it meant to sign away her parental rights. But Kyle was focused on Phoebe, who had somehow seen a way through this tangle and found a way to unknot the threads and restore order. From her quietly outrageous idea to get married, to seeing through Bianca's bad-girl exterior to the more complex—albeit still selfish—person inside.

He hadn't needed to blast forward with his background search on Bianca and level the field in a manner that would set bad blood between them for the rest of Nina's life. What more had he missed from Phoebe with his charge-ahead attitude that apparently kept him from slowing down long enough to pick up on important nuances?

He didn't know yet. But he looked forward to finding out one day at a time. Days and weeks and years of building a life and getting better as he learned more about her.

Starting today by telling his wife the most important detail, a detail his charge-ahead brain had wrongly plowed right over as insignificant. Once he got Phoebe alone, he intended to make sure that she heard, believed and never forgot.

He loved her.

Phoebe closed the door to Nina's nursery, Kyle behind her. She still couldn't believe they'd stumbled on Bianca's real agenda and it had been so easy to address.

Although now that she thought back, it made total sense. If Bianca had been after money, nothing could have stopped her from getting through to the Landis family. They should have realized that from the start. The talk with Ginger had helped her trust her instincts.

Bianca had seen the pieces differently than Phoebe would have ever guessed.

Phoebe leaned on the wraparound balcony,

tipping her face into the sea breeze. Kyle pulled up alongside her, his leg pressed against hers intimately.

Where would they go from here? More passionate sex that turned her inside out…only to find herself alone afterward? No, damn it, she'd learned. No more hiding in her dusty academic world. She would fight for herself, for this marriage, as firmly as she'd fought for Nina. Even if it took time.

She turned to face him, leaning an elbow on the railing. "Bianca surprised me today. She grew up. I'm relieved for Nina."

The cool breeze seemed to soothe the hot frustration of the last few weeks, easing the ache inside her. She just wished she could share some of that peace with Kyle.

"We accomplished what we set out to do." His voice wrapped around her with the same warmth it had that first night at his home-coming party.

Was it her imagination, or was there a hint of the old Kyle in his tone? She peered over at his strong profile as he looked out at the water.

"We accomplished it with a solution that's outside the box." Just like she hoped he would find for himself.

Like she hoped he might see for their future.

"You fought for us, for both of us, and I love you for that."

"If we keep thinking outside—" The word stuck on her tongue as her thoughts rewound and her heart picked up speed. "What did you say?"

That strong, handsome profile of his turned until he looked full-on into her eyes. "I said I love you."

Her jaw went slack. She'd been expecting

to dig in for a long haul, work to build a relationship that would lead to love, the way Ginger had found her second chance with her longtime friend. There were still so many pieces left to move.

"Kyle, are you sure? Wait, of course you're sure. You pride yourself on always being honest." Her head began spinning as fast as her heartbeat. "You were right that I was hanging on to the past. I was looking to recreate that, which is impossible. That was a unique love, just as my love for you is unique. By expecting this to be like the past, I almost missed how absolutely awesome the present could be."

Kyle frowned. His hands landed on her shoulders, steadying her. "Wait. Back up a second. Did you just say you love me, too?"

Oh, she had. And why hadn't she thought

to say that straight away to him? "Yes." She looped her arms around his neck, the truth of that simple fact shining through. "I am totally and completely in love with you. I know it's only been a few weeks. I'm the one who said things take time."

"I seem to recall you shouted it in the Aston." That gorgeous, lopsided grin of his returned, making her knees ridiculously weak.

"I did, didn't I?" Ah, but she would need that stubbornness to go toe-to-toe with her hardheaded Landis man. "My point is, I do love you. It came on me differently this time, but I know just as surely that this is real."

"Phoebe? Quiet, my love."

His love? She would never grow tired of hearing that. "Yes?"

"I should have realized sooner what was happening between us. God knows, you've rocked me more in a million ways than anyone has before from the first time I saw you, to the first time I kissed you, made love to you. Something about the way you handled things with Bianca finally got through my thick skull until I could see just how perfect you are, how perfect we can be together. I would be a damn fool if I let you go." His smile dug a dimple in his cheek. "I may have been slow on the uptake, but I'm not an idiot. I love you, Phoebe Landis, and I want to spend the rest of my life with you and our daughter and any other children we decide to add to our family."

"And I want to spend the rest of my life with you."

He tucked her closer against him, their bodies a perfect fit. "We'll start house-hunting here, for a place of our own."

A final problem tugged her with worries about long-term happiness. "But you love your job, the thrill of international dealings."

He tunneled his fingers into her hair. "I love you and Nina and the life we're going to have together more."

"I don't think I'll ever get tired of hearing that."

She arched up on her toes as he leaned down, his kiss wonderfully familiar and even better every time, as they built on the desire she'd felt the first time his sexy voice had stroked over her. How much more would she have to look forward to in the future?

His hands slid down her sides to loop low around her waist as he kissed along her jaw, his late-day beard a sweet abrasion against her skin. The scent of his aftershave mingled with the salty air, swirling inside her like dreams of their future unfolding. And just that fast an idea took shape inside those possibilities and plans.

Phoebe nestled against his chest, looking out over the ocean. "What if Nina and I traveled with you?"

His muscled arms tensed against her and he didn't answer at first, the waves rolling and receding while his heart thudded steadily under her ear. She stroked the hair at the nape of his neck. "Kyle?"

"I thought you would want the home and hearth here, stability for Nina."

So had she. At first. But she was learning more and more about thinking outside the box as she contemplated blending her life with Kyle's. "*We're* her security. And as you said before, we have options. We can hire an entourage of help so we never have to worry about finding sitters. We can afford to rent an entire house wherever we travel. Think outside the box for us, the way you do in your career."

"Your plan is definitely worth discussion." His face creased into a one-sided smile, his hands sliding intimately low down her waist. "We could always talk about it more on a long drive up the coast, since I decided to keep the Aston."

Possibilities flamed to life inside her, for now and all the years ahead. "Top down?"

She could already imagine the sea spray against her face, Kyle pulling over on a deserted stretch of beach…

"Whatever you want, my love," he promised. "I'll make it happen."

Epilogue

Nine months later

Ocean breeze caressing her bare shoulders, Phoebe draped her arms around Kyle's neck, her fingers toying with the hair at the nape of his neck. He wore it slightly longer now that he was no longer in the air force.

But they led a more spontaneous life overall these days as they traveled the world in his job as head of Landis International. Their latest stop? Lisbon, Portugal. They had renewed their marriage vows this afternoon with all the family gathered around the veranda at their rented waterside villa.

Her frothy off-white wedding dress twining around her legs, she tipped her face into the wind on this side of the Atlantic. "So we're really, *really* married now."

"I sure hope so." His hand slid between them to caress her stomach, which would soon start to swell with the baby they'd made two months ago.

Ashley and Matthew had a daughter now, baby Claire, who adored her older cousin Nina. Ginger and Hank Renshaw's grandparent nursery had just about expanded to a wing of cribs and toddler beds. They'd even added an in-ground baby pool and playground. But then, Ginger had openly admitted she was thrilled to entice her grandbabies over to spend time at Grandma's house whenever possible. Phoebe couldn't help but admire her mother-in-law's efforts when they always made her feel so very welcome.

Phoebe rested her hand on top of Kyle's, over their child growing inside her. "We should retrieve our daughter from her grandparents before they spoil her too rotten."

"It is her bedtime, isn't it?" He slipped his arm around her waist and steered her up the steps leading into the peach-colored stucco villa. Castle ruins nestled scenically on a mountainside in the distance. "I packed a new bedtime storybook for her, one about panda bears."

"She'll love it." Her grandparents weren't the only ones who enjoyed spoiling Nina.

"Next time we're in D.C. we'll have to take her to the National Zoo to see the giant pandas."

Phoebe found she enjoyed traveling with Kyle, and realized it wasn't a sacrifice after all with unlimited accommodations and a nanny. She continued to teach a class online, the perfect flexible career for a wife and mother on the go around the world. She was finally *seeing* the historical sites she taught her students about.

And she wasn't the only one enjoying her career. Bianca had actually struck it big as an actress after all—in Bollywood. She was totally enjoying her big-screen family in India. The Bollywood film industry had increased English-speaking productions and the viewers loved her. And of course Bianca loved being loved.

The money wasn't too shabby, either.

From all indications, she was very happy being a long-distance mother. She hadn't uttered a peep about the child-custody agreement and didn't even ask to see Nina half as much as she was allotted. They'd never even needed to roll out the incriminating images of Bianca, although they'd made sure she knew they had them. Since the nanny stayed with Nina during the few times Bianca came to the States to see her daughter, they knew the little girl was safe.

Nina seemed to see Bianca as more of an indulgent aunt who sent lavish gifts but rarely made an appearance. With that first sweet word, "Ma-Ma," uttered just for Phoebe, Nina had made it clear who she viewed in that role.

Phoebe paused in the wide-open double doors leading into the villa, inviting a cross-breeze. She turned her new ring around and around on her finger, the diamond-and-sapphire ring nestled alongside her diamond-studded band. "Do you know what I'm looking forward to most today?"

"What would that be?" He skimmed her loose hair back from her face, his gold band glinting in the setting sun. "I'll do my best to make it happen even better than planned."

She tucked against him suggestively, already envisioning exactly how all the pieces would go together once they were behind closed doors. "I can't wait for our wedding night. This time, we'll be celebrating on the same day that we said the vows."

"Now, that wish—" he smiled, dipping to graze a kiss at the corner of her mouth "—will be my absolute pleasure to fulfill again…and again."

* * * * *

millsandboon.co.uk Community

Join Us!

The Community is the perfect place to meet and chat to kindred spirits who love books and reading as much as you do, but it's also the place to:

- **Get the inside scoop from authors about their latest books**
- **Learn how to write a romance book with advice from our editors**
- **Help us to continue publishing the best in women's fiction**
- **Share your thoughts on the books we publish**
- **Befriend other users**

Forums: Interact with each other as well as authors, editors and a whole host of other users worldwide.

Blogs: Every registered community member has their own blog to tell the world what they're up to and what's on their mind.

Book Challenge: We're aiming to read 5,000 books and have joined forces with The Reading Agency in our inaugural Book Challenge.

Profile Page: Showcase yourself and keep a record of your recent community activity.

Social Networking: We've added buttons at the end of every post to share via digg, Facebook, Google, Yahoo, technorati and de.licio.us.

www.millsandboon.co.uk